THE LAST NEWSPAPER BOY IN AMERICA

SUE CORBETT

DUTTON
CHILDREN'S
BOOKS

DUTTON CHILDREN'S BOOKS

A DIVISION OF PENGUIN YOUNG READERS GROUP

Published by the Penguin Group • Penguin Group (USA) Inc., 375 Hudson Street, New York, New York 10014, U.S.A. • Penguin Group (Canada), 90 Eglinton Avenue East, Suite 700, Toronto, Ontario M4P 2Y3, Canada (a division of Pearson Penguin Canada Inc.) • Penguin Books Ltd, 80 Strand, London WC2R 0RL, England • Penguin Ireland, 25 St Stephen's Green, Dublin 2, Ireland (a division of Penguin Books Ltd) • Penguin Group (Australia), 250 Camberwell Road, Camberwell, Victoria 3124, Australia (a division of Pearson Australia Group Pty Ltd) • Penguin Books India Pvt Ltd, 11 Community Centre, Panchsheel Park, New Delhi - 110 017, India • Penguin Group (NZ), 67 Apollo Drive, Rosedale, North Shore 0632, New Zealand (a division of Pearson New Zealand Ltd.) • Penguin Books (South Africa) (Pty) Ltd, 24 Sturdee Avenue, Rosebank, Johannesburg 2196, South Africa • Penguin Books Ltd, Registered Offices: 80 Strand, London WC2R 0RL, England

CIP Data is available.

Published in the United States by Dutton Children's Books,
a division of Penguin Young Readers Group,
345 Hudson Street, New York, New York 10014
www.penguin.com/youngreaders

Designed by Heather Wood

Printed in USA • First Edition • 10 9 8 7 6 5 4 3 2 1
ISBN 978-0-525-42205-1

Were it left to me to decide whether we should have a government without newspapers or newspapers without government, I should not hesitate a moment to prefer the latter.

—Thomas Jefferson, 1787

TO THE BOYS, GIRLS, MEN, AND WOMEN WHO THROUGHOUT AMERICAN HISTORY HAVE RISEN BEFORE THE BIRDS TO BRING US THE NEWS,

AND TO BRIGIT, LIAM, CONOR, AND TOM, WHO GIVE ME GOOD REASONS TO BEAT THE BIRDS UP EVERY DAY.

—S.C.

THE LAST NEWSPAPER BOY IN AMERICA

New Carrier Prepares Customer for Takeover

"Impossible," Wil said, pedaling faster as the purple house came into view.

"What?" Sonny asked.

"Is she there *every* morning?"

"Who?" Sonny asked.

"You know who." A curve of sun rose behind him as Wil nodded in the direction of the house, where a scrawny blonde had sprung to her sandaled feet and was now skipping—*skipping!*—down the front walk. A silver camera on a cord strung around her neck slapped against her with each step.

"She went to art camp, but other than that, yeah, about every morning since school let out," Sonny said.

"Hi, Sonny!" Ann-Douglas, her hair pulled back in a ponytail and tied with a polka-dotted ribbon, waved at his brother.

Not only up, Wil thought, but up long enough to do her hair. "Does she realize this wrecks your time?" Wil whispered as he and Sonny braked to a stop.

"I can't wait to see if the paper ran my photo today," Ann-Douglas said.

Wil used great restraint to resist rolling his eyes. He wondered how much time she spent thinking up excuses to be awake, dressed, and waiting outside before six o'clock in the morning. The real reason Ann-Douglas was up, as everybody knew except maybe Sonny himself, was Sonny. He watched his older brother pull a copy of *The Cooper County Caller* from the canvas sack strung across his handlebars, smiling as he handed it over. "If it is, it'll be the most interesting thing in there, for sure," he said.

"Oh, Sonny, that's not true," Ann-Douglas said.

Oh, gag, Wil thought. She actually batted her eyelashes. Wasn't that out of style? "Ann-Douglas, you know you can sleep in and the paper will be right on your porch when you wake up," he said. "There's a crime blotter on the second page of the local section, and I've never once seen a report of newspaper theft."

She ignored him. "Would you like a cinnamon roll? They're almost ready." This was directed exclusively at Sonny.

Now Wil did roll his eyes. He might have been almost exactly the same age as Ann-Douglas, but they certainly weren't on the same wavelength. "We're right in the middle of delivering the papers, Ann-Douglas. This is our job."

"*Our* job?" Now she rolled her eyes. "It isn't *your* job until you turn twelve, I thought."

"That's tomorrow, Ann-Douglas," Sonny said helpfully. "Are you coming over? Junior's baking a cake. And you can try the Welcome Mat game again."

What was wrong with his brother? Is this why Ann-Douglas was always over at their house? Because Sonny provided her with excuses to drop by?

Ann-Douglas missed the invitation entirely. "But you'll

probably still help Wil for a while, right?" she asked. A note of worry sounded in her voice.

"I don't need any help," Wil said. For the past few days, he'd been working alongside Sonny, preparing to take over. Wil's family had lived in Steele since his great-grandfather founded the now-defunct hairpin factory, and all that time, one of the Davids had been the town's newspaper carrier. It was ironclad tradition to hand down the paper route to the next in line on his twelfth birthday.

That was tomorrow. Tomorrow, Wilson Glenn David the Fifth would be twelve. The route would be his. His quadriceps had strained and thickened cycling alongside Sonny. He'd suffered the aches proudly.

"Oh." Ann-Douglas did not hide her disappointment. Wil also noticed she hadn't even glanced at the paper. So much for dying to know whether one of her photographs had been published. Ann-Douglas fancied herself an artist. If she wasn't such a familiar figure at his house, constantly over to talk books with his mother, asking for advice on what she should read next, he might not even know what she really looked like. She always had her camera plastered to one eye, shooting close-ups of flowers or puppies. One time Wil saw her taking a picture of a fire hydrant.

She snapped her fingers. "I bet the rolls are done," she said quickly. "Wait one sec." She started toward her house.

"Sonny," Wil hissed urgently. There would be no hand-delivered papers or chitchat after today, that was certain. Tomorrow, Wil would keep track of his time with a stopwatch, to see how long it took him to do the route. His

father—known to everyone, including his own kids, as Junior—had held the record for decades. Wil was determined to break it.

"We better run, AD," Sonny said. "But I can smell 'em from here, and they taste like hot soup on a cold day."

She turned. From the look of confusion that crossed Ann-Douglas's face, Wil knew she was trying to puzzle out what Sonny had said. This was their chance. *"C'mon,"* he whispered firmly.

"Want to come back when you're done? I can warm them up again." Desperation was setting in.

Wil pushed off and cycled in a wide circle, waiting on his brother.

Sonny wavered, his feet resting on the pedals. He had impeccable balance, Wil thought, because the bike's equilibrium was off with the half-full sack of papers weighing down the front. Gravity would pull Sonny to the pavement if he so much as breathed unevenly.

"Sonny, people are waiting. . . ." Wil called.

"See ya." Sonny waved.

"Wait! What night are you going to the fair?"

"The fair is this weekend?" Sonny asked Wil.

"Let's *go,*" Wil whispered through gritted teeth. Arrrgh. Nobody should have this much trouble with a customer before breakfast.

Sonny hunched his shoulders in an I-don't-know gesture at Ann-Douglas. Wil was sure he'd crash now, but his brother righted himself in time for Dr. Feely's house, where the only thing waiting on the porch were hot-pink begonias in terra-cotta pots. Wil pulled a *Caller* from the sack on his bike and flung it with authority. It sailed true, arching over the flowers and onto the plank floor.

"Good one," Sonny said.

"That girl drives me nuts," Wil said when he was sure they were out of earshot.

"Nuts would make those cinnamon rolls even better."

"You're encouraging her."

"You would, too, if you'd had one. She puts this warm icing on them."

"I mean, you're too nice to her," Wil said, pulling another paper from his sack and whirling it toward the house where the town librarian, Ms. Parsons, lived. It smacked against the front screen door and fell back flat on the welcome mat. Rosie, her dog, started to howl. Wil made a mental note to land the paper closer to the front edge of the porch rather than the door tomorrow.

"Wil, my motto is, 'Don't bite the hand that tastes good,'" Sonny said, pulling the Gogginses' paper from his bag. "Try to throw this one as quietly as you can. She sleeps till noon in the summer." Mrs. Goggins drove a yellow half-size school bus, which picked up kids at the town green for the ride into Dweebville, without fail, at exactly 6:45 A.M. every morning of the school year. "Besides, it's too early to be less than nice."

Pointless, Wil decided. Sonny was simply incapable of seeing the consequences of being friendly to someone like Ann-Douglas. "It's one thing to be nice, Sonny. But you invited her over for *my* birthday."

"Heck, Wil, she was coming anyway," he said.

Cooper Cŏ. Fair to Open Thursday; New Thrills, Bigger Prizes

"You want to try Señor Lopez's house again?" Sonny asked.

Wil nodded and pulled ahead. Delivering the paper to Señor José Gilberto Lopez Lopez was the last, but the toughest, toss on the route. Sonny had explained that Señor Lopez had arthritis, so he took his medicine and had his espresso in his bedroom before coming downstairs.

"He likes to do the crossword puzzle with his coffee," Sonny had said, "so you gotta get him the paper right outside his bedroom door—on the balcony."

"You get it on the balcony without stopping the bike?" Wil had been slightly awed at first, but Sonny shared a tip he had gotten from Trace, the oldest of Wil's brothers.

"The secret is to throw ahead. Instead of waiting till you're right in front, throw from the edge of the property. You really have to let it sail to get it to rainbow over the railing."

Wil kept his eye on the balcony now as he threw the paper into a gentle high parabola. He had been thinking about parabolas because he wanted to learn geometry, but his mother said she wouldn't be able to teach him that herself. He knew he could find a class online, but he'd probably have to have a computer at home to take it. He wasn't going to be able to take a whole class on the computer he used at the library.

Señor Lopez's newspaper landed just inches from the sliding glass door.

"You look like you've been doing that for years, Wil," Sonny said. "Race you home?"

Wil picked up his speed, but let Sonny win. He was relieved his brother hadn't suggested they cycle back for cinnamon rolls.

"Y'know, I did forget about the fair," Sonny said as he leaned his bike against the back wall of the garage.

"How is that possible?" Wil asked. The Cooper County Fair was always held the last weekend of July. When Wil was younger he believed what his grandma Fleur told him—that it was scheduled in honor of his birthday. This year there was a new ride—the Wild Snake. Wil had read about it in the paper just yesterday. And there was a new midway game called Cover the Spot that had a $1,000 prize. Wil wondered how that worked, because he was sure the fair wasn't handing out that kind of money very often. Over the years, Wil had systematically figured out what the catch was at just about every one of the midway games. He considered it a personal challenge. Sure enough, they were all rigged, one way or another.

Sonny held the back door open for his brother, sniffing the air. "Dad's up."

"Up and gone down to the factory to trim the hedges with Mr. Bryant before it gets too hot to live," came a voice from the kitchen. Wil's mother was at the breakfast table, a book open before her, a mug of tea cooling by her right hand. "But he made you muffins."

"I could eat a moose," Sonny said.

"Muffins taste better." Wil got two plates from the cabinet and handed one to Sonny. "Where'd Junior get the blueberries? Mrs. Stinson have those?" Mrs. Stinson ran the market in what, for lack of a more accurate term, could be called "downtown" Steele—four blocks around the perimeter of the town green where all of Steele's commerce took place: the post office; the library; Heather's Hair Today, the only place to get a trim in Steele outside of somebody's kitchen stool; and the thrift shop. There were also a few shuttered storefronts that had once housed a luncheonette, a stationery store, and a coin-operated laundry. Once, before the hairpin factory closed.

"Ann-Douglas brought those by. She went to the U-pick farm in Coopertown yesterday with Judge Salzberg. It is so sweet how she is always thinking of us."

Wil believed he had set a new record for eye-rolling before breakfast. He needed to change the subject. "You're up early, Mom."

"I tried to stay awake to finish this book last night so I could be done with it, but look—" She flipped back a few pages and pointed to a dark spot. "Do you know what that is?"

"Tea?" Wil guessed.

"Do we want to know?" Sonny asked.

"That's drool. I fell asleep mid-paragraph and slobbered all over it."

"Can't you just stop reading if it puts you to sleep?" Sonny asked.

"You know I can't." Mrs. David wrote book reviews for a big magazine. Of course, there were no big magazines in Steele, but her college roommate Kim had become the book editor at one in New York City. The very first person she had hired was Magnolia David. Even in college, Magnolia would pick the longest checkout line at the cafeteria or at the registrar's so she could sneak in a few pages of whatever she was in the middle of reading. "To judge a book by reading less than all of it just wouldn't be fair."

"That reminds me, Mom," Sonny said. "Did you know the fair was this weekend?"

"It would be tough to forget," she said, winking at Wil. "After all, it was the fair that finally coaxed Wil out."

Another topic change, Wil decided. He had heard this story about his birth, which supposedly was early evidence of a stubborn streak, approximately one million times now. "It's been in the paper, Sonny."

"You *read* the paper?" Sonny asked.

"Don't you?"

"Everything in the newspaper but the comics is depressing. The only thing I read is whatever's on the middle third of the front page, above the fold. I read that story—I mean, that part of the story—a hundred times a morning."

"Sonny, it's not actually reading if all you do is glance at a fragment of a headline while it's spinning out of your hand," Magnolia said without looking up from her book.

He continued anyway. "One time, the only words I could read from the way the newspaper was folded were

'Mosquito Born.' That convinced me right there I didn't need to read more. I mean, how dull is a town where the birth of a mosquito is front page news?"

Magnolia stopped reading. "Sonny, was the word 'born' spelled with an 'e' on the end?" Conversations about words or grammar or spelling always got her attention.

Sonny shrugged. "It was dark out when I folded them, and when the sun came up the paper was folded right on the 'n.'"

"If it was 'borne' with an 'e,' which I'm sure it was, that 'borne' doesn't mean 'birth,' Sonny, it means 'bear.'"

Sonny threw his hands into the air. "That makes even less sense! There aren't any bears in Cooper County." He slapped his leg and then turned his hand to show Wil the red-and-black splatter on his palm. "We sure have mosquitoes, though."

Magnolia sighed. "Not the *birth* of a bear, Sonny—the mosquito was probably *bearing* a virus of some sort." She had actually closed her book by this point, with her finger holding her place.

"A sick mosquito? Well, shoot, stop the presses, then. I got a dead one right here."

Wil shook his head. Pointless. "Trace still sleeping?" He realized this was a silly question the moment he asked it. It wasn't even seven o'clock. Trace was seventeen. It could be hours before he appeared.

The distinctive sound of Junior's pickup truck rumbling into the driveway diverted Magnolia's attention from further instruction on the finer points of the English language. "That was fast," she said.

A door slammed. "Forgot the string trimmer!" a voice called, and then a moment later, Wil's dad appeared at the back door. "Any muffins left?"

"I'm trying to guard them so there's breakfast for Trace, but it's not looking good," Magnolia said.

"You boys want to whack weeds down at the factory? It's amazing how fast a place can look run-down in the summer."

Last year, Junior and Wil's grandmother Fleur had sold the Steele Hairpin Factory to Apex Hair Goods, a rival company. The factory had been losing money for years. Cheaper hairpins imported from other countries made it impossible to turn a profit, especially since the Davids believed that everyone who worked for them ought to earn enough to live on. They'd kept the factory operating long past the time it made economic sense, because closing it meant putting half of Steele out of work.

The prospective new owners had promised there would be no layoffs. One of Apex Hair Goods' representatives even told the town council they were considering an expansion to add a production line of barrettes.

So much for promises. Within a month of taking over, they shut down the plant.

Wil had never liked those two men from Apex. They had come to the house once looking to talk to Junior, but they wouldn't come in. They turned down pie—apple crumb—which Junior had baked himself. After the fact, Wil felt sure they never had any intention of keeping the factory open. They had bought the building, for next to nothing, just so they could put a pesky competitor out of business.

They lied, in other words. Wil hated liars as much as he hated cheaters. "I can work till the library opens," he volunteered. Wil went to the library on the mornings it was open, to play games online and surf the Web for new developments in aerodynamic research. He also checked his e-mail frequently, though he rarely received one that wasn't spam, except for the weekly e-newsletter from the Future Physicists of America.

The hairpin factory was just at the other end of the green. It was owned by the town now, which had taken possession when Apex Hair Goods, surprise, surprise, failed to pay its property taxes. Junior and some of the other former employees were keeping up the maintenance, hoping a new tenant would move a business in.

"Can I have another blueberry muffin if I go, too?" Sonny asked.

"How many have you had already?" Magnolia asked.

"Two."

"Oh, go ahead. But save one for Trace. It's not his fault he's a teenager."

So Sonny plucked another muffin from the basket, and Wil finished the last of his milk, already hoping there'd be something interesting to read from the Future Physicists of America. It was shaping up as another typically laid-back summer day in Steele, hot sun and blue sky. He and Sonny would help Junior till they were baked, then turn the hose on each other to cool off.

That was the plan, all right. Until the phone rang.

And then Wil's world, as he knew it, ended.

Phone Call Rocks World of Young Steele Resident

"Lemme speak to Sonny," a voice said sharply. Wil recognized it: Spike Matz, the circulation manager of *The Cooper County Caller.* He had been calling the house on newspaper business for as long as Wil could remember.

"It's for you," Wil said, handing the phone to his brother.

"Who is it?" Sonny asked.

Normally, Wil would have said "Ann-Douglas," but Spike's gruff tone had set off some kind of internal alarm. The circulation manager wasn't going to object to Wil getting the route, was he? Every David kid for decades had gotten the route. Heck, every paper ever flung onto a porch in Steele had flown from the hand of somebody named David. Even when the David boys were sick, or for the long stretches when Junior had gone off to college, Grandma Fleur had filled in. It wasn't just tradition; it was the most lucrative job a kid could get in Steele. Actually, other than mowing lawns or babysitting, it was the only job a kid could get. No adult wanted the route. The steep hill, narrow lanes, and low number of subscribers gave the Davids a lock on the job.

With mounting dread, Wil watched Sonny's face grow uncharacteristically solemn.

"Yessir." Sonny caught Wil watching him; he looked away.

There was no way Wil was not getting the route tomorrow. He practically had the money he was going to earn spent already! He had calculated, based on what Sonny collected in tips, how long it would take him to save enough to buy something he wanted desperately. He had even factored in that he wouldn't make as much as Sonny did, because Sonny had the kind of personality that made people want to give him money.

"I understand, sir," Sonny said before replacing the phone on its hook, his face pale and his usual smile nowhere to be seen.

"What'd he say?" Wil asked.

Sonny looked like he'd just taken a soccer ball in the gut. He seemed incapable of speech.

"Sonny?" Magnolia asked. The air had stopped moving in the kitchen. The second hand on the stove clock ticked to a standstill.

"What did he say, Sonny?" Wil asked, more insistently. Outside, the birds stopped chirping. Drivers stepped on their brakes, bringing their cars to a halt without knowing why. Wil realized he was holding his breath. "Tell me!" He knew it was bad news. Sonny had trouble telling people no even when that was the right answer.

"I can't believe this, Wil," Sonny said.

"Just say it, Sonny!"

"Spike says they're killing our route."

"What does that mean?"

"*The Caller.* They're ending home delivery to Steele."

Would-be Newspaper Carrier Reacts Badly to Change

"They can't do that!" Wil didn't mean to shout at Sonny, but he was stunned.

"He said it was nothing personal. 'A business decision.'"

Junior came into the kitchen. "Maggie, did you see what I did with that Asian cuisine story I cut out of the food section? I was thinking about pot stickers and a cucumber salad for Wil's birthday dinner, but I'm gonna need a few things from Stinson's." The only good thing about the hair-pin factory closing was that Junior finally had all the time to spend in the kitchen he wanted. Magnolia preferred reading to cooking anyway. "What do you think about pot stickers, Wil? They're like dumplings."

"Who can think about food?" Wil slumped into a chair.

"Something deflate his soufflé?" Junior asked.

"*The Caller* is ending home delivery to Steele," Sonny said.

"Run that by me again," Junior said.

"Spike Matz. He just called. He says the paper is doing away with the route through Steele."

"They can't do that."

"There's an awful lot of noise involved in whatever it is somebody can't do." Trace appeared in the doorway, looking groggy. His hair wasn't brushed, but he was dressed in his customary outfit—shorts, T-shirt, a pencil tucked behind one ear and a drawing pad slotted under his arm.

"*The Caller* is ending home delivery to Steele!" Wil told him.

"Does that mean there's no paper tomorrow?" Trace had hated doing the route when it was his turn, since what he enjoyed most of all in life—besides doodling on his pad—was sleeping in.

Junior and Wil both turned to Sonny. "Does it?" they asked at once.

Junior punched Wil in the arm just as Wil slugged Junior in the arm. "Jinx, knock on wood. You owe me a soda," they both said.

"Well, does it?" Trace asked. He did his level best to ignore the alarm every morning at four-forty-five, but he'd like it better if it didn't go off at all.

Sonny shook his head. "He said to give my customers thirty days' notice."

"Thirty more days of *brrring*." Trace tore a banana from a bunch on the counter and wedged it behind the ear without the pencil. Trace had exceptional hearing but unfortunately large ears.

"Is today Trish Myer's 'Life Drawing at Dawn' class?" Magnolia asked.

"Is there another reason a sane person would be up at this hour?"

Magnolia eyed the clock. "You've missed dawn by quite a stretch, Trace."

"I'll squint."

"*Hello!* Can we get back to the newspaper?" Wil said,

his frustration evident. "We only have thirty days to change their minds."

"How you gonna do that?" Sonny asked.

"Gotta go," Trace said, hurrying out of the kitchen.

Both boys looked at Junior, who trained his eyes on his youngest son. "Wil, this is a big company you're dealing with."

"I know," Wil said, although he admitted to himself that he didn't know a thing about the ownership of *The Caller*. He made a mental note to research it ASAP. Ms. Parsons would help him.

"Probably bigger than the one that bought the hairpin factory just so they could close it," Junior added.

"So?"

"So, I'm not sure even *you* are going to be able to change their minds."

"Well, not by hanging around here in our kitchen, I'm not. I mean, don't we need to at least know why? All these years and they just drop us? What does that mean, 'a business decision'?"

Junior looked thoughtfully at Wil. "You want me to call Spike?"

"We should go see him."

Junior sighed. "Okay. But John Bryant's waiting on me at the factory now. It'll have to be after lunch."

"Wil, have you considered that perhaps your customers would prefer to read something that's better written?" Magnolia said. Years earlier, Dr. Feely had suggested Magnolia stop reading *The Caller* because the number of typographical and grammatical errors raised her blood pressure to unhealthy levels. "An engrossing mystery or a riveting novel of historical fiction?"

Wil could not believe his mother had entirely missed the point. "I'll go myself," he said.

"Go where?" Sonny asked, but Wil had already slipped like smoke out the back door.

"Surely he's not riding his bike into Dweebville, Junior," Magnolia said.

"With Trace gone, this last muffin is going to go to waste," Sonny said.

Junior craned his neck out the kitchen window. Wil had already backed his bike out of the garage and hopped onto the seat. "Surely he is," Junior said.

"Sonny, go with him, please," Magnolia urged.

"Can I have this last muffin?"

"*Hurry*, Sonny," she said, nodding.

Magnolia closed her book, and Junior helped clear the breakfast dishes before going back to the hairpin factory. She was rinsing plates as Sonny pedaled down the driveway outside the kitchen window. Hopefully nothing would distract him before he caught up with Wil. Sonny was prone to sidetracks, and Wil would need Sonny with him if he got in to see Spike Matz.

The doorbell rang, and Magnolia leaned back from the sink to see who it was. "Come in, Ann-Douglas," she called. Actually, Magnolia thought, it was probably *Spike* who would benefit from Sonny's presence.

"Where's Sonny going?" Ann-Douglas asked, her arms laden with a stack of books. "He said he would pose for my morning-light series."

"Oh, I just sent him out with Wil," Magnolia said, drying her hands on a towel. "You done with all of those already?" she asked, taking the books to relieve Ann-Douglas's arms.

"Yep. I loved the one about the vampire who got to be homecoming queen, and the one about Eleanor of Aquitaine. How soon will Sonny be back?"

Magnolia put the books from Ann-Douglas on top of another stack in the front hallway. "Could be a while. Wil is upset with someone at the newspaper, and he has a tendency to argue his point until the other person collapses from fatigue."

"Is that why everyone calls him Wil of Steele?" Ann-Douglas asked.

"It is. He's had the nickname since he was born." Magnolia walked back into the kitchen to put her dish towel on the counter. "I'd offer you a muffin Junior made with those beautiful blueberries you brought us, but Sonny got to them."

"Oh, that's all right. I've already had two and a half cinnamon rolls. I'm close to exploding," she said. "How do you get a nickname at birth? I've never had one, and I've been alive for twelve years."

"Have you never heard this story?" Magnolia said, filling the kettle with water. "Tea?"

"Is there lemonade?"

Magnolia turned the kettle off and pulled two glasses from the cabinet. "Let's see. The year Wil was born we had one of the hottest summers on record. He was due at the beginning of July."

"But I thought his birthday was tomorrow—the twenty-eighth."

"It is. I tried everything to get him to budge. I even had my leaves read by Madame Prévu."

"Oooh, I have always wanted to have Madame Prévu read my leaves. What did she say?" Madame Prévu was Steele's Happy Medium.

"Told me what I didn't want to hear—that my baby would come when he was good and ready. Then I thought exertion might help, so I started walking up and down Wayout Hill with a book in the evening. Madame Prévu did think there was a slight chance getting closer to the moon might tempt him to appear."

"My father says you are the only person he has ever known who can read and walk without injury," Ann-Douglas said.

"It's not that hard," Magnolia confided. "If you don't pay any attention to the walking part, your instinct for self-preservation will take over."

"He says if read-walking were an Olympic sport, you'd have a gold medal."

"He is too kind. Should we take these out to the porch? It's cooler." Magnolia handed a glass of lemonade to Ann-Douglas.

"Anyway, it was the first night of the fair, and we were getting set to take the boys when I felt something stir. I was sure it was time."

"Was it?"

"No! The nurses said I wasn't in labor. But I was not leaving that place without a baby in my arms. He'd already changed horoscope signs on me. I wasn't going to let him switch months, too. I mean this baby was nearly four weeks overdue!"

"Wow. If he was a library book, they'd revoke your privileges for that."

"Exactly! So Junior tried to talk him out. He got even with my tummy and whispered promises about ice cream. Homemade vanilla with wet walnuts, which, by the way, no one likes but Junior."

"Did that do it?"

"No! Then I started telling him about the books I had put aside to read to him, stories with lavish illustrations, but that didn't get him to budge either." Magnolia sipped her lemonade. "Finally, Junior said, just off the cuff, 'Baby, if you don't hurry up, we're going to miss the fair.' That did it! Something shifted. I told Junior, 'Tell him more. Everything you know about the fair,' which to Junior means food. He went on and on about funnel cakes and fried dough and a green pepper that won a blue ribbon because it looked like Bill Clinton. He mentioned the pie-eating contest and the cotton candy and prizewinning jams. I literally felt Wil trying to kick his way out, screaming like he was sitting in the front car of the Cyclone with his hands above his head and his life flashing before him."

Even though it had been twelve years, Magnolia remembered the moment like it was a home movie she'd watched again and again. Wil weighed in at ten pounds, ten ounces, with a full head of fuzzy hair and one pearly tooth already sprouting in his pink gums. The hospital staff was agog. "Why, he's fully baked, isn't he?" the nurse said.

"Some babies would let their mamas cart them around forever, it seems," the orderly said.

"THAT is the most headstrong booger I've run across in thirty years of birthing babies," said the midwife. "You better come up with a strategy on how to deal with him now."

Good advice, as it turned out.

"So that was how he got his nickname—Wil of Steele, a baby so stubborn it took a county fair to get him to move," Magnolia said with a sigh. "So you can see why I'm worried about him."

"I can," Ann-Douglas said sympathetically. "It is good that Sonny's with him, then. Sonny's so agreeable."

"Oh, I'm not worried about Wil," Magnolia corrected. "I'm worried about the man he's going to see."

Would-be Carrier Demands Explanation

Sonny caught up with Wil as he was cresting the hill out of Steele. "You riding all the way to Dweebville?" he asked.

"Mom send you?"

"It's gotta be ten to twelve miles, Wil."

"Eight-point-two," Wil corrected him.

"Dang. How'd you know that?"

"I mapped it using one of those Internet sites."

"Just now?"

"A long time ago. I did it for a lot of places. It's eight-tenths of a mile from our house to the hairpin factory." Wil paused at the intersection of Wayin Road and Steele Highway to look for oncoming traffic. There wasn't any.

"What if we ride all eight-point-two miles and Spike's not in when we get there?"

"We'll wait."

"What if he won't see us?"

"He will."

"We could be there a long time."

"This is important, Sonny."

"Yeah, but we should've brought snacks."

# # #

When they reached Dweebville, they parked their bikes at the rack on Courthouse Square. Dweebville was the county seat, where the offices of *The Caller* and every other important institution, like the comic book store, were located.

Dweebville was an unfortunate name, but the founder of Cooper County had been a man named Dweeb Cooper, and he was the egocentric sort. He had named all Cooper County's towns—Coop de Ville, Beau Coop, Coopertown—for himself. All the towns except Steele, which wasn't a town until Wilson Glenn David the First built his hairpin factory there.

Inside the offices of *The Caller*, a receptionist sat behind a mahogany desk. She had on a headset with a little microphone curving along her jawline. Wil had an immediate urge to take it apart to look at the circuitry inside. If he'd been in a better mood, he'd have asked her if he could see it.

"We're here to see Mr. Matz," he told her.

"Is he expecting you?" she asked.

"He oughta be."

"If you don't have an appointment, I'm afraid—"

"We don't have an appointment," Sonny cut in, "but I just spoke with him on the phone. Is that an opal?"

The receptionist looked at her hand, which sported a slim gold ring with an oval white stone. "It's my birthstone," she said.

"I'm a Scorpio, too," Sonny said.

The girl, whose nametag read AMANDA, now smiled broadly. "October twenty-ninth," she said.

"You're a little older than me. I'm a boo baby," Sonny said.

"A boo baby?" she asked.

Wil was wondering where this conversation was leading but knew better than to get in Sonny's way when he was on a roll.

"Y'know—'Boo!'" his brother said emphatically, making little bursts with his fingers. "Born on Halloween."

"Oh, that's so cute!" Amanda squeaked.

Wil could almost see Sonny's spell work its effect. He had hypnotized Amanda. How did he do it?

"Let me see if Mr. Matz can see you," she said sweetly. "Have a seat. Do you boys drink coffee?"

"The only time I drink coffee is when I have a doughnut to dunk in it," Sonny said, "but thank you for offering."

"I'll check the break room. There are always doughnuts in there." She slipped off her headset. "Be right back." She went through a door behind her desk.

"You should think about becoming a magician," Wil said.

"Whaddya mean?" Sonny asked, plopping into an oversize armchair in front of a faux fireplace in *The Caller*'s lobby.

Amanda popped her head back through the open doorway. "Duh," she said, gently slapping her forehead. "Who should I tell Mr. Matz is here to see him?"

"Sonny David," he answered, "and my brother Wil. From Steele."

"Got it," she said, giving a thumbs-up sign.

This was probably something like the method Sonny used to get girls to do his homework, Wil thought. It was a trait Grandma Fleur said Sonny had inherited from his late grandfather Doc David. "Why, that man could sell hairpins to the Hare Krishna," she'd often brag.

Wil took a chair across from his brother and eyed the portrait of Old Dweeb Cooper, which took up most of one wall in the lobby. Dweeb had started the newspaper shortly after founding the county. Wil had read dozens of yellowed clippings from *The Caller* about the opening of the hairpin factory, the construction of homes for its workers, and the building of Steele's business district. He had even read sports stories about the factory's baseball team, the Steele Knights. His great-grandmother Mary David had apparently saved every newspaper article *The Caller* ever carried about Steele, meticulously pasting them onto the thick pages of several leather-bound scrapbooks. She was also a faithful diarist, no event too mundane to record in the notebooks she wrote in each and every day up until her death. Magnolia considered these diaries the family's most precious possessions and was thrilled when Wil asked to read them in order to write a history of Steele for his sixth-grade independent-study project.

"Mr. Matz is in a meeting," Amanda said, delivering a tray to the coffee table with two steaming mugs, cream, sugar, and a plate piled high with several different kinds of doughnuts—double chocolate, powdered sugar, glazed. "It may be a few minutes. I didn't know how you took your coffee, so I brought everything. Help yourselves."

"You are too kind, Amanda," Sonny said, plucking a doughnut from the stack.

"No problem," she chirped, returning to her desk.

"Don't forget to dunk it in your coffee," Wil said.

"What? And ruin a good doughnut?"

"It just dawned on me who you are." Amanda reaffixed her headset. "You're the carriers in Steele, right?"

"I am today," Sonny said. "But Wil is tomorrow."

"I've heard about you." This time, she looked directly at Wil. "Aren't you the one who kept running away from school?"

Wil wondered, not for the first time, if this story had actually *been* in the newspaper. It was one thing that everybody in Steele knew it, but how in the world had they heard it in Dweebville?

"Actually, he's homeschooled now. It was just kindergarten he kept running away from," Sonny said. "Our mother would drop him off at school, but he'd escape by midmorning. The teacher even thought about nailing the windows shut and locking the door from the inside, but that was against the fire code."

"Why would anybody run away from kindergarten? Those cute plastic scissors, the smell of Play-Doh, naptime—"

"It was boring," Wil cut in, hoping that would put an end to this particular discussion. Magnolia had taught Wil how to read before he started school, and he was constitutionally averse to napping. It wasn't that he didn't like it. He simply couldn't do it. Eventually, Magnolia gave up trying to send him back to school. Wil applied for a library card, and his mother agreed to homeschool him. Wil was an excellent student so long as the subject suited him. He liked geography, science, and mechanics.

"My parents say they should've seen it coming," Sonny continued. He was looking directly at Amanda, so he missed seeing the death stare Wil was aiming at him. "When he was maybe two, he spent the whole summer in the buff 'cause he decided clothes were a bother."

"Sonny, nobody cares about this story," Wil grumbled.

"I do!" Amanda said with evident delight. Most of the people who visited *The Caller* were placing classified ads or were angry about something the paper had printed. They rarely told her funny stories.

"Our mother tried everything, but he figured out how to undo buttons, zippers, safety pins. Heck, she even used duct tape on his diapers, but Wil—"

At that moment, Wil took another doughnut from the plate and slotted it into Sonny's mouth mid-sentence.

"Uf, gut," Sonny mumbled. "Cimmamim."

Fortunately, the door behind Amanda opened before Sonny could swallow, and Spike Matz, a wiry man with a waxed shine where his hair should have been, emerged.

"Hey, Sonny," Spike said. "Climbed out of that deep hole just to see me?"

Wil got up, crossing the lobby to the reception desk. "Mr. Matz, we're here to talk about *The Caller* ending home delivery to Steele."

"Who are you?"

"Wilson Glenn David the Fifth. I'll be twelve tomorrow."

The significance registered with Spike. "Well, Wil, I'd explain the whole thing, but I assure you it's over your head."

"Try me."

"Son, I'm just following orders."

"Are you gonna come out here and talk to us?" Wil demanded.

"Take it easy, Wil." Sonny had finished his doughnut and come up behind his brother.

Spike sighed and walked around Amanda's desk. He gestured for Sonny and Wil to follow him to a spot under the portrait of Old Dweeb.

"There's no point in me telling you any of this, but I will because I've known your daddy for a long time. You know Double-G sold the paper, right?" Double-G was Dweeb Cooper's great-great-grandson, the current publisher of *The Caller.* Also known as Dweeb the Great. "Well, these new guys are big on cutting costs and increasing profit. They've got him slashing down to the bone around here. They even outsourced the payroll department to some firm in Truth or Consequences, New Mexico, so we get paid once a month now instead of every other Friday—to save on the cost of printing checks. There was a near riot over that."

"Truth or Consequences is the name of a real town?" Sonny asked.

"They ought to worry about businesses that stop handing out payroll checks, period," Wil said, his thoughts on his dad and the hairpin factory.

Spike nodded. "Anyway, we had to look at every route in terms of whether it was worth the cost of getting the paper there—are these the people our advertisers are trying to reach and, if not, was the route profitable in its own right? We were able to make a case for every route but the one through Steele. It's just too small, and too remote."

Wil couldn't believe his ears. "So that's it? You can't make more money off us, so we don't matter?"

"This isn't a charity, young man. We can't put out a newspaper if we can't make money doing it, can we? And these new owners, their issue is 'quality' circulation, because that's what the advertisers want. Those big-box stores that sell electronics or office supplies or discount pet food? If you don't live in a zip code that's within five miles of their store, they figure you're not shopping with them anyway, so why should they be paying to advertise their stuff to you?"

Wil understood this. Most of the advertising circulars that came with the Sunday paper were for stores he had never been inside. "I thought the newspaper was supposed to be a public service," he said.

Spike rubbed his hand across his scalp to smooth down hair that wasn't there. "It wasn't my decision, boys."

"Well then, whose decision was it?" Wil demanded. "Let's talk to him."

Sonny put his arm around Wil's shoulder. Wil shrugged it off.

"I'd be disappointed, too, if I were you," Spike said.

"Whose decision was it?" Wil felt his cheeks flush, his anger rising.

Spike flashed his eyes upward at the portrait of Dweeb. "The publisher's. But he said if he didn't do it, somebody at News, Inc. would."

"We'd like to talk to Double-G, then," Wil said. "You can't just stop delivering the newspaper to a whole town. It's, it's . . . un-American!"

"Double-G is at the new headquarters, in Cincinnati," Spike said.

"We're not waiting until he gets back from Cincinnati, Wil." Sonny worried that might be the next suggestion his brother made. "We'd die of hunger."

"I can give him a message if you want," Spike said.

Wil considered this. He wasn't sure what he wanted to do, but he wasn't willing to share the details with Spike. Something in his manner made Wil reluctant to trust him.

"I'll write a letter to the editor," he said. One of Grandma Fleur's hobbies was writing letters to the editor. She was always protesting something. Before she had started traveling to save the planet, she wrote *The Caller* almost every day, but a lot of the time it was to complain about *The Caller* itself. They had stopped printing her letters after a while.

"That's an idea," Spike said. "You can both write."

Sonny physically recoiled at the suggestion. "Oh, no, not me. I take writing off for the summer."

"Tell ya what." Spike turned his head in Amanda's direction. It appeared she was talking into her headset. He waved his hand at her before swiveling his attention back to Wil and Sonny. "Did you both get the five-dollar-off coupon for the 'ride-all-day' wristband at the fair?"

"No, sir! Where was that?" Sonny asked.

"It was in the *paper*," Wil replied.

Spike looked over toward the reception desk again, where Amanda had finished taking a message. "Amanda," he called. "You still have those coupons?"

Amanda opened a desk drawer and rifled through the

contents before producing a wad of small rectangular papers.

"Let me give you a bunch of these for you and your friends," Spike offered.

"Let's go, Sonny," Wil said. He would not be bought off with discount rides at the fair.

Amanda scrambled around her desk and handed the coupons to Sonny, who crammed them into his front pocket. "Thanks for the doughnuts, too," he said, winking. She smiled in return.

Wil had already walked out and was unlocking his bike by the time Sonny caught up with him. "That went about as well as it could have, don't you think?"

Wil squinted into the sunshine, tears swimming at the rims of his eyes, and pedaled off without answering.

Steele Resident Suffers Worst Birthday Ever

Wil rose before the alarm clock rang. He hadn't slept well. His mind kept turning over the meeting with Spike, and the conversation that had followed with his parents, who thought it was futile to talk to Double-G himself.

"It's a business, Wil," Magnolia said. "And they get to choose how to run it."

"But what about Señor Lopez and his crossword puzzle, or Mrs. Stinson taking the sports section with her so she can read it at the store? How about all the kids who won't get the comics anymore? Don't they care?"

"Businesses don't stay in business if they lose money," Junior said. "Look at the hairpin factory. Maybe if we'd switched to barrettes like Madame Prévu suggested, we'd still be open."

Wil thought even horoscopes were ridiculous, but it was impossible to ignore the fact that Madame Prévu's predictions were often correct. Wil figured she was a good guesser.

"It's not that we're not sympathetic, Wil," Magnolia said. "It's just that this is like trying to fight City Hall."

"City Hall's involved in this, too?" Sonny asked.

"That's just an expression," Wil said.

"But that reminds me, Maggie," Junior said. "Those guys from the county Economic Development Council are coming down tomorrow to take a tour of the factory."

"Do they have a tenant?"

"Well, if they do, they haven't mentioned it to me, but at least they're coming. I've been trying to get on their radar screen for months."

Now Wil swung his legs over the side of his bed and squinted out the window. The sun wasn't up yet, but he dressed without turning on the light so as not to wake Sonny or Trace. The brothers shared a room fashioned from the sloped-ceiling attic, their beds pushed against the wall with the one small window, and a night table slotted between each narrow mattress.

He slipped downstairs and out the back door to the garage. He was early, but he wanted out before anybody else was up. He didn't want help this morning.

A month's worth of summer heat rose from the pavement as he pedaled up Wayout Hill to meet Manny Morrison, the driver who brought *The Caller* to the road above Steele. An arc of the sun was now visible in the east, scaling the mountains beyond Dweebville.

As he crested the hill, he spotted a crow at the corner of Steele Highway and Wayin Road, where Manny always left the papers if he arrived before Sonny did. If Wil had overslept, the newspapers would be waiting for him, bound with a plastic strap he'd slice in two with the Swiss

Army knife Grandma Fleur had given him for his tenth birthday.

"This is an *authentic* Swiss Army knife," she'd boasted. "Bought it in Gstaad."

Wil had beaten Manny there, but the crow had beaten them both.

"Don't worry," Wil said, leaning his bike against a tree. "I'm not going to take any of your worms." The bird caw-cawed in annoyance and flew off into the rising sun.

Wil grabbed a handful of pebbles. Sonny had a game he played while he waited for the papers—trying to hit the O in STOP so that it nicked the paint. A glance at the sign revealed how good Sonny's aim was—the red paint inside the O was thoroughly pockmarked. Wil flicked his wrist and—*ping!*—hit the center of the O on his first try.

He couldn't believe how unlucky he was. This should have been his day. He sidearmed a second rock. Another direct hit.

He *had* to talk to Double-G, make him see how unfair it was to stop delivery to Steele. He pinched a flat pebble between his forefinger and thumb and hurled it. The sound of rock hitting metal reverberated in the heavy morning air.

Darn! What was the use? Dweeb didn't care how long Wil had waited, that he had his twelfth birthday circled in red permanent marker on the calendar. He didn't know Wil had dog-eared several pages in a catalog, because he knew precisely what he would buy when he finally had some money.

Wil didn't just want a laptop computer. He *had* to have one. The Steele branch of the Cooper County library had only two public computers and they often took turns working. Wil always tried to get to the library the moment its doors opened but, still, if he had his own computer, he could do so much more. He'd found sites with online design tools that he could use to simulate ideas he had about aerodynamics and engineering. There were message boards he'd had to hurriedly read through, full of postings by people who he knew would be able to answer questions he had if only he had time to have a whole conversation with them. There was a ton of stuff to do that couldn't be done in the twenty minutes he was allotted if somebody else was waiting, and someone almost always was.

How could he earn enough to get a laptop now, without the route? He couldn't! He threw another rock so hard he flinched, afraid it might ricochet in his direction.

Wow, he thought, moving closer for inspection. I wonder if Sonny ever *bent* the sign with a rock. There was a depression right in the center of the O and a pimple on the back side where the rock had dented the metal. Nah, he decided. Sonny never got as steamed as Wil felt now.

The rumble of an approaching truck caught his attention. Wil slapped his hands together to shake off the dust from the rocks.

"Morning, Wil." Manny shut the engine and stepped down from the cab. "You on your own?"

"Hey, Manny," he answered. "Yeah, just me."

"That's a fine happy birthday." Sonny had introduced them to each other last week.

"I can do it myself. At least for a month."

Manny was at the back of the truck, rolling up the gate to reveal his cargo: stacks of *Caller*s in plastic-strapped bundles. "Uh-oh. Spike already call you?"

"We saw him yesterday."

In the dim light, Manny checked the slip on the top of one stack. "Heavy today." He dropped the load on the ground near Wil's bike. They landed with a *thud* that sent up a dusty plume. "Grocery inserts."

"Thanks," Wil said, slipping his hand into his pocket for his knife.

"What did Spike say?"

"He said the route through Steele isn't profitable enough to make it worthwhile."

"If that don't beat all." Manny pulled the gate back down. "You're better off finding something else, Wil. There's no future in newspapers. This month it's Steele, but it ain't long before *The Caller* will go the way of the drive-in movie theater. Everybody'll get their news from TV or the Internet."

"You really think that, Manny?"

"Learn to type, Wil. Sure wish I had."

"I know how to type. I need money. There's no other job for kids here. Heck, there's no job for my dad." He looked up at Manny, worried he shouldn't have brought his father into this.

"Plenty of dads doing your job now. In fact, you're the only kid left in my territory. It's all grown-ups in minivans. Heck, Wil, you might be the last newspaper boy in America. End of an era."

Wil had sliced through the plastic binding and began folding the papers in thirds, securing each with a thick rubber band. He wasn't interested in being the end of an era. "Not if I can help it."

Manny climbed back into his cab, chuckling. "Attaboy, Wil. Go get 'em."

Wil glanced at his watch. Before yesterday, before the phone call and the meeting, Wil thought his focus today would be on how fast he could do the route. Sonny's average time was in the low forty-minutes. Wil knew he could beat that. Not that Sonny would care. (Sonny would shake his hand.) Or Trace. Trace had refused to keep track of his time, but it was safe to say he'd never challenged the record held, for more than twenty-five years, by Junior.

In his day, Junior could routinely finish in a lot less than forty minutes. His best-ever time was thirty-six minutes, eight seconds.

Without trying, Sonny had gotten under thirty-eight minutes a time or two. There was a cartoon show he liked to watch on Saturdays at six-thirty, so if the truck was late he'd put on the gas to get home for that, but Wil . . . Wil wanted to be the new record-holder. Years ago, his grandfather Doc had predicted he would be.

"You got everything it takes, Wil. You're steady on the bike, you got a strong arm, and your aim—well, your aim is the best I've ever seen. Better than your father's, but don't tell him I said so."

Doc had said this with Junior standing right there, so he winked as he said it.

Wil's heart had swelled with pride. The thought of that moment now filled him with fury. He'd never get good enough in a month to beat the record. He needed practice to shave seconds off the time it took to circle every street in Steele.

The key was to take advantage of the hill—coasting down Wayin Road to the far end of Steele, and doing the homes behind the hairpin factory first. After that, opinion divided. Junior knocked out the homes on Mane Street (it had been Main Street, but seeing as it dead-ended at a hairpin factory, the spelling had been changed long ago) and then wove a route through the culs-de-sac. Sonny liked to weave first and save the straightaway down Mane for last.

Wil had planned to try both, and time each segment.

He was thinking about all of this as he flew down Wayin Road, letting the breeze cool his skin as he held the handlebars steady. The first paper was always delivered to Mrs. Stinson, not because she was the mayor, but because she lived on the edge of town and, when the factory had been running, she'd open her market early so people coming to work could get coffee and a pastry. She would take the newspaper with her so she could read it after the morning rush.

Wil pulled a *Caller* from the sack and slowed a bit to toss it. He turned his head to watch it land on the porch, skidding to a stop just inches from the welcome mat. Mrs. Stinson waved at him from the door.

"Come by the store when you're through, Wil," she called. "I've got a little something for you."

He waved back before reaching for the next paper. Everybody knew it was his birthday. Dang it! A tear fell from his eye, dotting the pavement. He'd have wiped it away but he couldn't take his left hand off the handlebar, since he was using his right hand to throw. He flung Judge Salzberg's paper with a little too much oomph and it banged hard against the front door. Wil winced, and took a deep breath to get his focus back. He tossed Ann-Douglas's into her outstretched arms, gently though, so as not to hit her camera. Guess she didn't believe Sonny would sleep in and miss whatever she was baking. He tossed a biscuit from his pocket to Oscar, the Suttles' dog, to distract him while he flung their newspaper onto the porch. "Otherwise," Sonny had warned, "he thinks he's supposed to retrieve the newspaper for you, and then he'll chase you all the way down Edinburgh Street to give it back."

Yes, that first morning, Wil's birthday, his first day as the new carrier in Steele, a day he had circled in red for the better part of a year, every paper hit its target. Wil should have felt happy or proud. Instead he felt defeated.

It was a feeling, Wil realized, he'd never had before.

Phone Call Delivers Greetings from Abroad

Wil knew by the aroma that hit him when he opened the back door that his father was up. Junior always made chocolate crepes with whipped cream for birthday breakfasts.

"Happy birthday, son," Junior called from the kitchen.

Wil muttered, "Thanks," just as the phone rang. A call this early could be from only one person. After Doc died, Grandma Fleur began traveling pretty much full-time, not as a tourist, but with any relief agency that would take her. She'd dug wells in northern Nigeria, been to Indonesia with the Red Cross after the tsunami, tutored in Appalachia. At the moment she was with Friends of the Planet in South America, but wherever she was, she always had trouble remembering what time it was in Steele.

"That's probably for you, Wil." Junior lifted the edge of the crepe with his spatula to peek at the underside. "Thirty more seconds," he said, turning down the heat.

Wil tossed his shoes into the basket and hurried to answer the phone. "*Buenos días*, Grandma Fleur."

"And *Feliz Cumpleaños* to you, Wil. This is awful early to have the route done. You didn't beat Junior's record on the first day, did you? Doc always said you'd be the one to do it."

"Just up early, Grandma."

"Rarin' to go, I expect. I didn't think you'd be home yet, so I was calling to tell your daddy to make sure you check your e-mail at the library. I sent you an e-card."

"*You* have a computer now?"

"Heck, no. I sent it from a cybercafe in Valparaíso. It sure don't have the charm of a postcard, but it's easier to find an Internet connection these days than a post office."

"Does this mean you have an e-mail address now, too?"

"It's *FleursAbroad@sudamerinet.com*." She spelled it out for him. "I sent an attachment, too. Something I want your mama to proofread for me. Print it out and bring it home, will ya?"

"Sure, Grandma."

"You haven't asked a single question about Chile."

"How's Chile?"

"How's Wil, is what I want to know. It's your birthday north of the equator, too, isn't it? What's with the glum tone?"

"It's nothing." He'd been hoping he could get off the phone without telling her the news.

"My earlobe's tingling, Wil. Out with it." Fleur's earlobe vibrated whenever somebody lied to her, so Wil knew the jig was up. He told her the story.

"Oh, that gets my knickers in a knot, Wil. What they're saying is people in our town don't matter."

"It's so unfair! I tried explaining that to Spike, but he doesn't care. So then I asked him to let me talk to Dweeb the Great, but he says he's in Cincinnati. So I guess I'm gonna write a letter to start with."

"Don't some of them customers care?"

"I haven't told them yet." Wil took a seat at the table with the phone still pressed to his ear.

"Well, the newspaper bean counters sure aren't going to change their minds unless somebody convinces them to, and I doubt even Wil of Steele can turn this tide by himself."

Junior slid a plate of crepes in front of Wil and whispered, "Bone in your teeth." Sonny had started French in middle school and firmly believed this was what was said before meals in Paris. Magnolia had tried to correct his pronunciation, but Sonny could not be moved. Eventually his family gave up and adopted his version.

"Your daddy making crepes?" Fleur asked.

"Yeah. They're ready."

"I can smell 'em through the phone. Eat up before they get cold. But, what about a petition, Wil? Or a sit-in in *The Caller*'s lobby. You got to let 'em know who they're dealing with." Suddenly there was static on the line and Fleur's voice cut out. "You there, Wil?"

"Yeah. Your voice cut out for a minute."

"What I was saying was that with your persistence, I've always had a secret hope you'd go into cancer research. We'd have a cure in a New York minute."

Wil had to laugh at that. "Okay, Grandma. Thanks."

He clicked off the phone and looked down at his plate. A sit-in? How did that work? Would he get arrested? He might feel better about things if it meant going to jail.

He picked up his knife and fork. Wil had never *not* been hungry for chocolate crepes before. If he didn't eat them his father would be heartbroken, so he sliced off a small piece. Maybe he could circulate a petition when he went door-to-door tomorrow, collecting the weekly subscription fee. Grandma Fleur was right! He couldn't just let *The Caller* stop delivery without a fight.

Junior set his own plate on the table and took the seat facing Wil.

"Where's Mom?" Wil asked. What would he do if no one signed his petition? Maybe his mother had a point, too. Maybe people would rather read something other than the newspaper.

"Read-walking, before it gets too hot. If you pass her somewhere on the way to the library, tell her I need confectioners' sugar? Two pounds'll do."

Wil nodded while he swallowed a bite. His appetite surfaced as soon as he tasted the warm, gooey crepe.

"I'm afraid we don't have much of a present for you. But I got a coconut cake going now, and we'll do the Welcome Mat game, of course."

"Do we have to?"

Junior's fork clattered to his plate. "Did you just say, 'Do we have to?'"

The Davids had been playing the Welcome Mat since Junior could walk. When most babies turn one, they get a stuffed bunny or one of those pretend lawn mowers with plastic balls that pop as it's pushed. Junior's present was a Frisbee. Frisbees were new back then. Doc immediately saw their potential as a training tool for a future newspaper flinger.

"Ain't he a little young?" Fleur had asked when Doc stood Junior on the sidewalk in his diaper and urged him to sidearm the Frisbee toward the front porch.

"Heck, no," Doc said. "It takes years of practice to get this right. I wish I'd started at his age."

Baby Junior bounced the Frisbee onto the concrete. "Goo bah," he said, clapping his hands.

"I say you're pushing it." Fleur had let the screen door slap shut on her way inside to get the cake.

That was how the Welcome Mat game began. Each David got a Frisbee on his first birthday. Before cake was served, all of them would line up on the sidewalk and attempt to wing the plastic disk onto the porch, as close to the welcome mat as possible. Doc would have the kids try various techniques—low to the ground, a high lob, right-handed (clockwise) and left-handed (counterclockwise)—because, ultimately, they'd be aiming at other front porches, on different sides of the street, and the obstacles at each house on the route were all slightly different.

"You have to learn to take the trajectory into account," he told them. This was on Sonny's fifth birthday. Trace was still four years away from taking over the route.

"Tra-jek-tree?" Wil was two.

"His first multisyllable word!" Magnolia hugged him.

"That means the arc of the throw, Wil," Doc said. "Say you need to clear a railing. You gotta throw it like a rainbow, so it arcs over the railing but drops sharply. That way you don't break the front window."

"Tra-jek-tree!" Wil said. "Tra-jek-tree!"

"Ain't he a little young for words with more than one syllable?" Fleur asked.

"You're never too young for multisyllable words," Magnolia said.

After everybody could land the Frisbee on the mat, Doc made them try the same trick with newspapers. He'd save a stack of ten for each.

Junior had mastered landing the paper on the welcome mat by age nine.

Trace never embraced the art of it. He broke two flowerpots on his tenth birthday (Magnolia switched to window boxes as a result) and, on his eleventh birthday, hit the cat, who'd been asleep under a rosebush. Doc was so alarmed by this that poor Trace spent his entire eleventh year riding the route alongside Junior, practicing.

Sonny, on the other hand, had an easy, natural flair. He was hitting the welcome mat with the newspaper by age eight. By the time he took over the job from Trace—something Trace referred to as "the happiest day of my life so far"—he could complete the entire route without ever coming to a stop, except on Sundays. (Sunday newspapers are a whole 'nother matter.)

But nobody was a more precocious hurler than Wil.

Wil hit the welcome mat on his third birthday.

"Will you look at that?" Doc said. "Give him two pieces of cake!"

But Wil wasn't content to have mere talent. In first and second grade, he insisted Magnolia school him in aerodynamics so that, by third grade, he was an expert on the forces that cause a Frisbee—and a newspaper—to move through the air. He could calculate the role wind would play in accuracy. He practiced folding the paper so that it formed a mostly flat plane—with a gentle arch.

"If you look at the Frisbee from the side, you see the rounded edge resembles the shape of an aircraft wing," he explained to Trace, who, at that point, had been doing the route himself for two miserable years.

"Airplanes have engines, Wil."

"I know that, Trace, but the curved surface of the wing is what generates lift," Wil told him.

"So?"

"Well, if you fold the paper so that it curves slightly, you'll create the same kind of lift. You could even put a little English on the spin, so the paper would land in an upright position, leaning against the front door."

"You're making this a lot more complicated than it has to be, Wil."

Trace never listened to him, but Wil persisted. "If I were you, I'd stack the papers in the sack so that the curves face you. That way, you don't have to turn them upside down before tossing."

"You need a hobby, Wil. Collecting baseball cards or something."

Naturally, Wil loved the Welcome Mat game. He'd won six straight years—a streak stretching back to Sonny's eighth birthday. That year Wil hit the mat ten times, besting Sonny's score of nine winners.

But at the moment, he found he couldn't summon

any enthusiasm for the game. "I just don't feel like it today."

Junior's shoulders drooped as he studied his son. "It's a family tradition, Wil," he said.

Delivering the newspaper was a family tradition, too, Wil thought. But he didn't say that. It wasn't his father's fault that *The Caller* had decided the people of Steele didn't matter. And, besides, he was fixated on what Grandma Fleur had said: He had to fight back.

Steele Boy Inks Outraged Message to Publisher

After breakfast, Wil cycled to the library. He waved at Ms. Parsons, who was on the phone, before heading to the computer. He logged on and clicked the mouse to open his e-mail program. Grandma Fleur's message was the only one in his mailbox.

To: WilofSteele@topmail.net

From: FleursAbroad@sudamerinet.com

Subj: ¡A dozen Feliz Cumpleaños!

Well, you've done it. Made it to year 12. Congratulations. You'll have been up and finished the route by the time you read this. I sure am proud you're carrying on this family tradition. Doc, wherever his soul has taken root, would be mighty pleased to see the baton (so to speak) passed to you. He always said you had the best fling of his grands.

I sent you a gift—something I found when I was helping Friends of the Planet renovate their new headquarters—an old Royal typewriter. They got computers here now like they do everywhere else so they let me have it for the sweat equity of cleaning out an office nobody's used since General Pinochet was in grade school.

You'll have it taken apart and put back together in a jiffy, but I think you'll like looking at its innards. I took the cover off myself and it kinda reminded me of a piano with all them arms and keys. It's going on the slow boat, but will make it home before I do.

I've finished my stint here. I'm off next to the Pantanal in southwest Brazil. There's birds and plants going extinct there every ding-dong day, so there's not a moment to lose, if you know what I mean.

Con amor, (that's how they say "with love" here)
Su umbrella (That's "your grandma" in Spanish. I might be spelling it wrong.)

P.S. I know a little tech whiz like you can figure out how to print out a copy of this letter that the nice señor here in this café attached to this e-mail for me. ¿Can you ask your mama to proofread it and then send it back? ¡Moochas gracias!

P.P.S. ¿Ain't it funny how south of the equator the exclamation points turn themselves upside down and plant themselves at the beginning of the sentence as soon as you type one at the end? ¿Will wonders never cease?

Wil downloaded the attachment from Grandma Fleur and sent it to the printer. It was a letter to the editor of *The Satellite Valley News*—the big city paper in the next county owned by News, Inc., the same company that had just bought *The Caller.* Out of the corner of his eye, Wil noticed Zach Griggs chatting with Ms. Parsons. Zach was often waiting to use the computer by the time Wil finished his allotted twenty minutes. Wil logged off and called, "Finished here," to Zach, who waved in acknowledgment.

Wil grabbed *The Satellite Valley News* from the rack and settled into one of the cushy chairs by the window. The front page had stories about a hostage situation in Russia, a traffic pileup on the interstate that had killed two, and a drought in the Midwest that was affecting crop prices. Sonny was right. A lot of what was in the newspaper was worrisome or worse.

But not the stuff Wil read. He pored over the articles about weather and scientific research. He liked to study the maps, even if what they depicted was precisely where some rebels were fighting, or the exact spot a plane had crashed. He remembered a map that showed the path of a hurricane—how it had led him to the big atlas Ms. Parsons kept behind the reference desk. He wanted to know the names of all the little dots in the newspaper map—

places that were really inhabited islands in the middle of the sea. Wil wondered what that would be like, to live surrounded by nothing but blue water, hundreds of miles from the next bit of land. Would you feel stranded? Was it scary, or was it awesome?

But Wil had to admit that he usually skipped the stories about apartment fires and boat sinkings. Was it that he didn't care? No. But he wasn't sure how knowing that stuff helped in any way. It could make a body feel hopeless. Grandma Fleur had always said that caring about other people and places was the first requirement of being a citizen of the world. Maybe he'd been wrong. Maybe he should be paying more attention to the peace process in the Middle East, or famine in sub-Saharan Africa, because now, would he ever even get a chance? *The Cooper County Caller* had decided that Wil, and his family, and his friends, and his neighbors didn't count enough—*didn't make them enough money*—to keep them in the news loop. If steam could have come out of Wil's ears, the library would have been able to charge admission to a sauna.

He folded the *News* in half and tossed it on the table in front of him. From the newspaper rack he took the morning *Caller.* He was already composing what he had to say in his head. He put the newspaper on his chair, then crossed the room.

"Ms. Parsons, do you have a piece of paper and a pen I could borrow?"

"Isn't today a very special day for you, Wil?" She smiled at him.

"Kinda."

"My newspaper was right on the top step when I let Puddin'head out this morning," she said, fishing through her desk drawer. She withdrew a pad and a ballpoint pen. "Will these do?"

"Yes, ma'am. Thanks."

"Happy birthday, Wil. I really admire the way you're here every day, even in the summer when the other homeschoolers take time off."

"Thanks, Ms. Parsons," Wil mumbled. He didn't have it in him to tell her about *The Caller* ending service to Steele. He'd have to tell everybody tomorrow, on collection day. Unless. Unless he could figure out a way to get Double-G to reverse the decision.

Wil laid the pad and pen on the table and opened the paper. There was another ad for the fair on page 3—rides, ribbons, and in big type, $1,000 GRAND PRIZE, at the Cover the Spot game on the midway. Wil wondered again what the game could possibly entail. It must be something so difficult no one could ever win. But then why would anybody play?

He found the newspaper's masthead, which listed the names of the editors, the address, and a little paragraph with guidelines on submitting Letters to the Editor.

Lookit that. You could send them by e-mail.

Wil roughed out what he wanted to say, then waited for Zach Griggs to leave. There was no one else in line, so he hopped back on and typed his letter.

To: publisher@coopercountycaller.com
From: WilofSteele@topmail.net
Subj: Home delivery to Steele

Dear Mr. Cooper:

My name is Wilson Glenn David the Fifth. I am the newspaper carrier in Steele. I learned yesterday that you plan to discontinue delivery in our area.

You are a nitwit, Mr. Cooper. It is no wonder your parents called you Dweeb.

Writing that second paragraph was the most fun Wil had had since he'd turned twelve. He read it twice before dragging the Delete key across the whole thing. Then he went back to what he had scrawled on the paper Ms. Parsons gave him.

To: publisher@coopercountycaller.com
From: WilofSteele@topmail.net
Subj: Home delivery to Steele

Dear Mr. Cooper:

My name is Wilson Glenn David the Fifth. I am the newspaper carrier in Steele. I learned yesterday that you plan to discontinue delivery in our area.

Did you know that, here in Steele, everyone gets the paper? Television reception is weak here, and there's no cable. People depend on The Caller to know what's happening outside our town.

You run a newspaper. Your job is to keep people informed. Do you really want to keep the residents of Steele from knowing who is running for governor? How the Pirates did? What the weather will be like? What's going on with Garfield?

Put yourself in our shoes, Mr. Cooper. How would you feel if somebody decided the place where you lived wasn't important enough to get the newspaper anymore?

Sincerely,

Wilson G. David V

Wil reread what he had written and hit Send. It might not do a bit of good, he thought, but he felt better for having done something.

Newspaper Flinger Notches Record-breaking Win

The boost Wil got from sending the e-mail to Dweeb the Great didn't last the length of time it took him to cycle home. He passed the grocery without stopping, not wanting to face Mrs. Stinson—or any of his other customers.

He wondered how long it would take the publisher to reply. Too bad Grandma Fleur's birthday present wouldn't be in the day's mail. A dismantling operation was just what Wil needed to get his mind off *The Caller.* Instead he spent the afternoon getting glummer and glummer. He cycled back to the library just before closing time to check his e-mail. No response from Dweeb. They had e-mail in Cincinnati, too, didn't they? Now Wil wondered not when but if the publisher would ever reply.

At dinner, he pushed his pot stickers around his plate but never actually took a bite.

"You gonna eat those?" Sonny asked. "They're good dipped in whatever that brown stuff is."

"Ginger-hoisin sauce," Junior said.

"Ginger Hoyson?" Sonny asked. "Is she the lady who invented it?"

"Invented what?"

"The brown stuff."

"No, no, Sonny," Magnolia explained. "The *name* of the brown stuff is ginger-hoisin sauce. It's a Chinese marinade."

"Oh, so like Ginger was the inventor's girlfriend?" Sonny speared a pot sticker from Wil's plate. "Dad, you should name one of your recipes for Mom."

"He already has—those fruit tarts, remember?" Trace interjected.

"Oh, yeah—Maggie Pies. You haven't made those in a while, Dad."

"Those are the ingredients, Sonny," Junior added. "Ginger *and* hoisin sauce."

"Really? All I remember was the custard. So creamy." Sonny pointed at Wil's dinner. "I'll take those if you're not going to eat 'em."

Wil tipped his plate over Sonny's, and the pot stickers slid off.

"I could make you something else," Junior offered.

"Okay. I'd like to be a twelve-year-old who *has* a job."

"I meant something else to eat, Wil."

"No, thanks."

Junior and Magnolia exchanged worried glances. "I guess we shouldn't be surprised, Wil, but you're taking this news about *The Caller* awfully hard," Magnolia said.

Wil shrugged and moved his fork around his empty plate.

Junior broke the silence: "Okay, I guess we're ready for the game, then, huh?"

"I'm gonna pass," Wil said, lifting his plate from the table, pushing in his chair.

"That's it. Take his temperature," Trace said. "He's obviously ill."

"Wil, honey, I'd say I'll make sure they let you win, but you always win anyway," Magnolia said. "You once told me it was the highlight of your birthday."

Wil usually loved playing the Welcome Mat game, which he and Sonny renamed the *Dobro došli* game when Fleur surprised them two years earlier with the gift of a new doormat that said *welcome* in Serbo-Croatian. It was a souvenir from a trip to Bosnia-Herzegovina with Landmine Action!, a group that was working to protect people from accidentally blowing themselves up.

But nothing was going to cheer up Wil today. Or maybe ever.

"C'mon, Wil," Sonny said. "You can pretend the *Dobro došli* mat is Spike Matz's backside and you're smacking him with a paper."

Wil couldn't help but crack a smile at that.

The doorbell rang as they were clearing the dishes. "I wonder who that could be," Wil said without looking up.

"Hi, Mrs. David!" Ann-Douglas chirped from the other side of the screen door. She had another stack of books, and her camera was slung crosswise across her chest so that it hung at her hip.

"Sonny, let Ann in, please," Magnolia said. "Put those anywhere you can find a clearing, Ann-Douglas," she called. "Did you get through all of those since yesterday?" Ann-Douglas sampled many of the books Magnolia received and let her know which ones were worth reading.

"No, these I found today when I was looking for Dorothea. She was hiding because she had to go to the vet." Dorothea was Ann-Douglas's cat.

"Anything good?" Magnolia and Ann-Douglas had met at the library several summers earlier when Ms. Parsons had asked Magnolia to give out the awards for the summer reading contest. Magnolia was the closest thing Steele had to a celebrity, since she worked for a big magazine that wrote about celebrities. Wil used to enter the summer reading contest, too. In fact, the year Magnolia met Ann-Douglas was the first year he had ever finished second. Ann-Douglas won by a landslide.

"There are two I would finish if you didn't need them back right away," Ann-Douglas said.

Wil read quite a bit, but wouldn't pick up any book with a cover that was pink, sparkly, or featured women's body parts. It was amazing how many books had just body parts on the cover—feet, legs, torso. Wil had learned this functioned like a label warning him he would not be interested in the contents. His mother had tried to draft him as her "co-reader," as she now called Ann-Douglas, but there were too many books he would never waste his time on—novels about foreign women in previous centuries or dorky romances set in big cities, stuff like that—and not enough about the things he was interested in, like irrational numbers or the science of flight.

"Can you stay for cake?" Magnolia asked. "It's Wil's birthday."

Ann-Douglas pretended to be surprised, Wil thought.

"Ooh, I can take photos! If we wait till twilight I can override the flash, boost the shutter speed, and take a photo of Wil blowing out his birthday candles using just the available light! I've been wanting to try that!"

Wil thought she should have tried it at her own birthday, a month ago.

"Well, how 'bout the Welcome Mat game right now, then, AD?" Sonny asked. "You wanna play?"

Wil barely suppressed a groan. Next they would be adopting Ann-Douglas.

"Is that where you try to get the newspapers by the door?" she said.

Sonny nodded. "Wil could use some new competition."

"Oh, Sonny, you know I throw like a girl," Ann-Douglas said.

Wil could not suppress his groan.

"I'm going to skip this year's competition," Magnolia said. "You go ahead, Ann-Douglas, and then we can talk about the books you've gotten through."

Ann-Douglas would be here for hours, Wil thought. Magnolia seemed to like nothing more than hearing Ann-Douglas's thoughts on books. His mother rarely asked for *his* opinion, and had been known to *actually start to nod off* when he tried to tell her about the latest controversial issue being discussed on the Future Physicists of America Listserv or the ins and outs of a new online game he'd played.

As expected, no one really challenged Wil for the Welcome Mat crown. All ten of his newspapers not only reached the mat, four of them landed horizontally, covering the words *Dobro došli*—the equivalent of a bull's-eye. Sonny and Junior both hit the mat eight times. Despite her protests that she had a handicap, not having been brought up in a newspaper-flinging household, Ann-Douglas came in fourth, hitting the mat three times and the porch twice. Sonny retrieved the tosses that landed in Magnolia's azalea bushes, and Wil had to restrain himself from gagging at the fuss Ann-Douglas made over Sonny's chivalry. He wondered if she was tossing them errantly on purpose just to get Sonny to wait on her.

Trace announced that, henceforth, he would compete in an alternate version of the game with a new target, and successfully landed six of his ten attempts in the storm gutter of the porch roof. He was climbing a ladder to retrieve them when Junior and Magnolia went inside to get cake, plates, forks, and a pitcher of pink lemonade.

"Bombs away!" Trace dropped the papers on Sonny, who was trying to head them soccer-style onto the porch. It wasn't working.

"Dang," Sonny said when another paper thudded to the ground. "That's harder than you'd think."

"A soccer ball is heavier and retains more of its initial velocity during flight," Wil told him.

"The rest of us speak English, Wil," Ann-Douglas said.

Wil ignored her and spoke directly to Sonny. "Spherical objects are more aerodynamic."

"So it would be easier to get newspapers on a porch if they were round?" Trace asked, dropping another newspaper on Sonny's head.

"Maybe, but the newspapers would roll away."

"Time to make a wish, Wil." Magnolia was holding the door open for Junior, who carried a tall cake, alight with twelve thin candles.

"That's one hairy cake," Sonny said.

"Not hair, Sonny, coconut," Junior corrected.

"How come coconuts in pictures are always brown?"

"That's the *outside* of the coconut, Sonny," Magnolia explained. "The flesh is white."

"Coconuts have flesh? And hair on their insides? I bet that tickles."

"Better hurry, Wil," Junior said. "Wind's picking up."

There was only one thing Wil wanted. He didn't believe in wishes, but he said it silently in his mind anyway, then inhaled deeply.

"Wait! Sonny, would you move that broom from the wall behind Wil?" Ann-Douglas asked. "It's cluttering up my background."

"You're not going to be able to see anything behind me in this light, Ann-Douglas," Wil said.

"Trace, stand here with me to block the wind," Junior asked.

"And, Wil, can you move that lock of hair off your forehead?" Ann-Douglas said.

"No," he said, drawing in a big breath.

"Wait! I haven't adjusted my shutter speed!" Ann-Douglas said.

How did I get roped into this? Wil wondered.

"Okay, I'm ready," Ann-Douglas said.

"Are you sure?" Wil asked.

"Go, Wil," she demanded.

He snuffed out all twelve flames with a single breath.

Magnolia hugged him. Junior took a large knife from the back pocket of his jeans and cut five thick slices and one skinny one.

"Ooh. This is pretty good," Ann-Douglas said, turning the camera to show the screen to Sonny. "Look at the tonal variation in Wil's face!"

Sonny squinted at the small image. "I think that's a birthmark, Ann-Douglas."

Junior handed the first slice of cake to Wil. "Your mom and I have decided you need a night out, Wil. For your birthday, we're going to treat you to opening night at the fair tomorrow."

"We need to help you out of this funk," Magnolia said. She looked at Junior lovingly. "After all, it was mention of the fair that got you born to begin with."

Wil took his cake and settled back on the porch swing. "We have money for the fair?"

Junior handed plates to Ann-Douglas, Trace, and Sonny. "Sure we do. We always have something put aside for a rainy day."

Sonny looked skyward. "If it's supposed to rain, maybe we should wait till Friday."

"Oh, Sonny," Ann-Douglas said, giggling. "That's just an expression. The weather's supposed to be beautiful."

Magnolia licked her fork. "By 'rainy day,' they mean the possibility of some trouble or difficulty in the future."

"Who could have trouble at the fair?"

"Not at the fair, Sonny. In life. It's an old phrase. First used in America by Benjamin Franklin, who probably picked it up when he was ambassador to France. The French expression is *'Gardez une poire pour la soif,'* which means, 'Keep a pear for thirst.'"

"Hmm. According to Fleur, they drink wine in France, not pears."

Wil cut in. "Speaking of Fleur, she sent me an e-mail with a letter that she wants you to proofread, Mom."

"Fleur's got e-mail now?" Junior was slicing himself another piece of cake. He always took a very thin slice first so he could have seconds. "She's something, ain't she?"

"What's the letter about, Wil?" Magnolia asked.

"It's a letter to the editor of *The Satellite Valley News*. I didn't read it, though."

"Some new bug up Fleur's bottom," Junior said.

Wil saw confusion cross Sonny's face and he knew he'd have to step in now or the conversation would go to a place it shouldn't while people were eating. "I'll get it after dinner. It's in my library book."

"So how about the fair, Wil?" Junior asked.

Sonny chimed in. "I've got money, Wil. And you'll get some tips tomorrow."

Collection day. Wil realized he'd managed to put it out of his mind.

"That's right nice of you, Sonny," Junior said. "Plus, you gave me an idea at dinner—I'm going to enter my Maggie Pies in the bake-off. The blue ribbon comes with a hundred-dollar prize. You got more of those blueberries, Ann-Douglas?"

She nodded. "I'd love to go to the fair tomorrow," she said. "I just can't decide what to enter in the photography contest. I've had three of the pictures I took of Sonny on his bike matted and they're my favorites, but other people like my series on found objets d'art."

"Do you want to bring them by and let us vote?" Magnolia asked.

"Well, if we're all going to go tomorrow, I'll enter something in the art show," Trace said.

"Wil, I have a great idea," Magnolia said. "Why don't you enter your paper on the history of Steele in the writing contest?" She had judged the contest the previous year. "If you'd entered last year, you might have won, and not because you knew the judge."

"Why?" Ann-Douglas asked.

Magnolia rested her fork on her plate, pausing to choose her words. "Let's just say that if I had been made to read one more poem written in a singsong rhyme, I might have set fire to the whole stack," she said. "I ached for a well-researched piece of nonfiction by the time I got to the end."

"Is it open to kids, though?" Ann-Douglas asked.

"There's one category for kids under thirteen, if I remember correctly," Magnolia said. "What do you think, Wil?"

Wil was staring off into space, not paying attention to his mother's conversation with Ann-Douglas. "Sure," he said, not sure at all what he was agreeing to. "Mom, do we have a copy of the Declaration of Independence?"

To: WilofSteele@topmail.net

From: customercare@coopercountycaller.com

Subj: Your message of July 28

Date: July 28

Dear Mr. Wilofsteele:

Thank you for contacting The Cooper County Caller, Satellite Valley's news leader, now with more classified listings online than any other newspaper in the South Central Downstate region.

We are reviewing your comments and hope to get back to you shortly.

Please note: This e-mail was sent from an address that cannot accept incoming e-mail.

Best regards,

Luke Ryan

Vice President, Customer Care

* * * * * * * * * * * * * * * * *

Satisfied Readers Are Our No. 1 Priority!

* * * * * * * * * * * * * * * * *

FIND THE PERFECT NEW HOME IN OUR ONLINE REAL ESTATE SECTION

* * * * * * * * * * * * * * * * *

LOOKING FOR WORK? CHECK OUT OUR ONLINE JOB HUNT SITE—www.paycheckthisFriday.com

Newspaper Boy Collects Money—and Signatures

Thursday had always been Collection day. Sonny promised Wil they'd go together the first week so Wil would know what to expect at each house. Some customers left an envelope under the mat. Some had run out of money since the previous payday—especially since the hairpin factory closed—and would need an extra day or two. One or two made sure they were nowhere to be found every Thursday afternoon.

"Lotsa people tip a dollar, so, on a good week, you can clear fifty bucks easy," Sonny had told Wil a lifetime ago.

"Fifty bucks?" The figure had staggered him. It would take Wil a whole year to save that much otherwise.

"It's worth a dollar to most folks to let us cycle up that hill," Sonny added. "'Course there are some not-so-good weeks. You gotta pay for the papers, whether you collect or not, so if a customer gets a few weeks behind, that's out of your pocket."

This Thursday, there was also the matter of delivering something else: bad news.

"I'll ask for the money," Sonny said. "You tell them what's going on."

"That's the hard part, Sonny."

"I dunno know. Getting three-seventy-five out of Kristin Zwicklbauer is no walk around a piece of cake."

"Walk in the park."

"That either."

Sonny had technically been the carrier for five-sevenths of the week, but he offered to split the tips fifty-fifty.

"Is that out of pity?" Wil asked.

"Heck, no. Figuring out five-sevenths of something is work. I take math off for the summer." They braked in front of Mrs. Stinson's and leaned their bikes against a telephone pole. "You got the book?"

Sonny had bequeathed Wil a slim black ledger. It was spiral-bound and could open to add pages. It was the same book Junior had gotten from Doc on his twelfth birthday, and most of the customers listed then were still customers now, except for the ones who had died or moved. The cover was worn, and the book had a gentle curve to it—the shape of the David boys' rear ends, because each stowed it in the back pocket of whatever pants they wore on Thursday. Wil pulled it from his own pocket now and held it up.

"Then we're ready," Sonny said, gesturing for Wil to go first.

Wil patted his shirt pocket to check for his pencil and headed up the walk and the two wooden steps of the front porch. He rang Mrs. Stinson's bell and moved back.

No one answered, and Wil felt something close to relief. He had a tight grip on the ledger, into which he had slipped a folded sheet of lined paper—the petition he had written the night before. Magnolia had found him copies of the Declaration of Independence and the Constitution in an encyclopedia, and Wil used them to write his own words of protest. He had scratched out several different versions while listening to Magnolia and Ann-Douglas on the porch going on and on about a new biography of Jane Austen, whoever she was. Finally satisfied, he had carefully copied the sentence he'd come up with onto the top of a blank sheet:

> We the People of Steele, in Order to Remain an Educated and Informed Citizenry, do Hereby Protest the Cancellation of Newspaper Delivery Service to Our Town.

He had made up his mind to ask for signatures after checking his e-mail that morning. A stupid auto-reply.

But now Wil felt chicken. He had practiced a short speech, but it was one thing to say it in his head, another to deliver it to whoever answered the door.

"Maybe she's still at the store, or over at Town Hall," Sonny said. "We'll circle back."

They coasted to the next stop, where there was an envelope with Sonny's name on it attached with a clothespin to the lid of the mailbox. Wil was getting increasingly nervous with each empty house. The Robertses were next, and Wil didn't really know them at all. He was worried about whether they would want to sign his petition.

"Sonny, is it okay if we start at the end and do Señor Lopez Lopez first?" Sonny had told him Señor Lopez was one of his favorite customers, real smart, and a good tipper.

"Fine by me," Sonny said.

Señor Lopez was sitting on a rocker on his front porch, doing the acrostic with a ballpoint pen. "It cannot be Thursday already, can it?" he said when he looked up to see Sonny and Wil ride up his walk on their bikes.

"*Buenos días,* Señor Lopez," Sonny called as the boys made their way toward the porch. "This is my brother. He's taking over the route."

"This one has the same name, too?" Señor Lopez asked. All the Davids were named Wilson Glenn David because, over time, Wilson David the First had come to regret letting a clerk at Ellis Island take the *off* off his original name, which had been Davidoff. He had impressed on his son—perhaps a little too much—the importance of preserving the family name. Of course, what this meant was they all had to have nicknames so they could tell which ball cap was whose, or who was being summoned to set the table. Trace had gotten his nickname from Grandma Fleur, who was home from one of her fact-finding missions when he was born.

"Well, we can't call him 'Three,'" Junior said. They were watching through the plate glass as a nurse at Cooper County General gave Wilson Glenn David the Third his first bath.

"He sure don't like water," Fleur said. "He might spit out a lung with all that crying."

"You got any ideas, Ma?"

"For starters, I'd bathe him as little as possible."

"I mean about the name."

"How 'bout Trace?" she said. "That's Spanish for three." Grandma Fleur had learned to count to ten in four languages, including Quechuan, which she had picked up while working as a poll watcher in Latin America. Unfortunately, she couldn't spell in any of them and thought the Spanish word for three—*tres*—was spelled like the English word for drawing something using very thin paper.

"One of those country singers has that name." Junior turned the word over in his mouth, testing it. "Trace. Trace David. I like it. Let's check with Maggie."

Wilson Glenn David the Fourth was saved from a life of answering to "Cuatro" by Fleur's decision to volunteer with a group building irrigation systems on the Ivory Coast the month before he was born. For weeks, he didn't have any nickname at all. Junior called the baby "son," when there was occasion to call him anything. Finally, Magnolia added the "ny."

"It matches his disposition," she said.

Doc objected till Junior told him—in a blinding flash of spontaneous thought—that "Sonny" was short for Wilson.

"A nickname from the back end?" Doc asked. "Can that be a good idea?"

Whether it was or not, it stuck.

And then came Wil.

"Yes, Señor Lopez, the same name," Sonny said, "but we call him Wil."

"That, finally, is sensible," Señor Lopez said. "Let us see how sharp he is. Wil, I offer you the same challenge I often make your brother. I will give a bigger tip if you can solve my puzzle."

Wil snickered, but he was game. "Okay. Shoot."

"Name a word in the English language in which every vowel appears in alphabetical order."

"*Facetious.*"

Señor Lopez smiled broadly. "*¡Muy bien!* I am impressed."

"Dang! How'd you know that, Wil? I haven't gotten the answer right in almost three years of trying to solve Señor Lopez's riddles."

"If you'd been homeschooled by our mother you'd have known it, too."

"Technically, the most correct answer is facetious*ly*," Señor Lopez said. "But I will pay anyway, because the letter *y* is not universally considered to be a vowel. It is a vowsonant."

"What the heck's a vowsonant?" Sonny wanted to know.

"A letter that can be a vowel or a consonant—the hermaphrodite of the English language, if you will."

"I won't, but thanks anyway," Sonny said.

Wil smiled. "I've never heard of a vowsonant before," he told Señor Lopez. Occasionally he did wonder if there were some gaps in his education that his mother had neglected to fill, but he didn't think she'd have missed a chance to lecture him on a *whole category* of letters.

"That's because the coinage of *vowsonant* is mine. I made it up." Señor Lopez looked very pleased with himself. He reached into the pocket of his jacket and extracted a ten-dollar bill from his wallet. "Keep the change."

"Thank you, sir!" Wil fished his pencil from his pocket and put a check mark next to Señor Lopez's name in his ledger. He saw the petition sticking out from his book but hesitated.

"Er, Wil," Sonny whispered, "you forgot to tell him . . ."

"Forgot to tell me what?" Señor Lopez asked.

Wil blurted it out before he lost his nerve: "*The Caller* is ending home delivery to Steele, sir."

"What does this mean?"

"It means, in twenty-nine days, I won't be bringing you the paper every morning."

"Who will be bringing it, then? Is there another boy with the same name after you?"

"No, sir. *The Caller*'s owners have decided to end home delivery to Steele," Wil said.

Señor Lopez studied Wil's face hard. "That can't be."

"I'm afraid it is."

"That is an outrage!" Señor Lopez stood suddenly and then winced. He steadied himself on the arm of his chair. "No one will stand for this. There will be a hue and cry!"

"Hugh who?" Sonny asked.

"I certainly hope so, Señor Lopez," Wil said, ignoring Sonny's question for fear of a long sidetrack. "Would you be willing to sign my petition?"

"You got a petition?" Sonny asked.

Wil slipped the sheet from his ledger and placed it in Señor Lopez's outstretched hand.

"Hand me my reading glasses please, Sonny," Señor Lopez said, gesturing to the table between them. "I could have trouble getting up again if I bend down myself."

"Sure thing," Sonny said.

Señor Lopez slotted the glasses onto his face with one hand and quickly scanned Wil's petition. "Now I need the pen, Sonny."

"Here you go," Sonny said.

Wil plucked a hardcover book from the table. "Here, lean on this."

Señor Lopez put the petition atop the book to sign his name. He wrote it big, and in a very fancy style:

José Gilberto Lopez Lopez

"There," he said, clicking off his pen. "Now even King George will be able to read it."

"King George is involved in this, too?" Sonny asked.

"Good luck to you, my boy!"

"Thanks, Señor Lopez!" Wil said, a bounce in his step as he and Sonny headed back to their bikes. "We'll keep you posted."

Psychic Forecasts Struggle for Last Newspaper Boy in America

The next three customers eagerly signed Wil's petition. Mrs. Kelley was steamed. "Do they think we can clip coupons from the TV?" she grumbled.

"Disgraceful," Judge Salzberg muttered as she scratched her name across the sheet. She was actually a retired judge and only went into Dweebville when the dockets got full. "I'll write a letter myself, but good for you boys for taking action!"

Ann-Douglas, who lived next door to Judge Salzberg, was there, photographing the judge's geraniums. "Can I sign, too?" Ann-Douglas asked, and Wil was feeling so upbeat, he let her, without hesitation. He nearly flew off the judge's porch, his mood lifted by everybody's righteous indignation at *The Caller*'s decision. By the time he and Sonny got to Madame Prévu's, he was so pumped he felt almost . . . happy.

Madame Prévu was in her yard, digging as Wil and Sonny came up the walk. *"Bonjour, mon beau rayon de soleil,"* she tootled, without turning around.

"Hey, Madame P.," Sonny said. "You trying to grow windows?" Close up, the boys could see that Madame Prévu was dropping shiny, broken shards of glass into a deep hole.

She cocked her head. "Did you hear that?"

"What?" Sonny said.

"That barking." Madame Prévu sighed and moved to her right, turning over a new patch of dirt with her spade. "If you hear a dog barking, you must fill in the hole you are digging and start a new one."

"Whatcha burying, Madame P.?" Sonny asked.

"I dropped a hand mirror." She scooped up the pieces in her gloved hands and hurriedly transferred them to the freshly dug hole. "And I see I have waited too long. You have bad news." She fixed her eyes on Wil.

"Wow, how'd you know that?" Sonny asked.

"The price for that rag is going up again?" she guessed.

"No, it's going down. Permanently," Wil said.

"Tell me more. You are the brother, no?"

He nodded. "*The Caller* is ending home delivery to Steele."

"Hmm." She turned back to the dirt, filling in the hole and patting it flat. "Only bad news for some." She stood, removing her gardening gloves before brushing the wrinkles from her skirt. Above her front door Wil noticed a horseshoe affixed to the wall, prongs up. "But very bad for you, correct?"

"Right."

"Pourquoi?"

"I just took over the route," Wil said.

"Ah, fortunes reversed." She climbed the steps to her porch, where she retrieved a beaded purse. "And when does this change take place?"

"Never, if I can help it. I have a petition here . . ."

Wil offered her the sheet with the other neighbors' signatures. Madame Prévu tucked her purse into her skirt pocket, then took the petition, holding it in both hands as she scanned the words. Wil noticed she had rings on every finger, including her thumbs. She reached behind her head and pulled a pencil from her hair bun, unleashing a cascade of brown corkscrew curls that fell past her shoulders. Madame Prévu signed the petition, then handed it back, staring hard at Wil. "When is your birthday?"

"It was yesterday." Wil realized he was having trouble breaking eye contact with her. Her gaze felt almost magnetic. He had an urge to leave but was unable to move. He didn't feel scared, just not totally in control.

Madame Prévu twisted her hair into a rope and used the pencil to knot it into a bun again. Then she closed her eyes, splaying her fingers across her temples. Her hands looked like spiders wearing jewelry, Wil thought. He stole a glance at Sonny, who met his eyes nervously. Wil was just about to jerk his head to signal that they should tiptoe backward down the walk and leave Madame Prévu in her trance when her eyes opened wide. She walked to her front door and, on tiptoe, removed the horseshoe from its hook above the door.

"Come closer, Wil."

He wasn't sure he wanted to, but his feet moved toward her almost involuntarily.

"The petition will not work," she said, tipping the horseshoe right side up, directly over Wil's head. "Stand still. I'm spilling some luck on you."

Sonny chuckled. "That horseshoe looks empty to me, Madame P."

"I assure you, it is not." Madame Prévu returned the horseshoe to its place.

Wil wouldn't admit this to anyone, but he *had* felt something tingly, like goose bumps on his skin, when Madame Prévu held the horseshoe over his head. "If you don't think the petition will work, then why are you giving me luck, Madame Prévu?"

"The petition will not work, but you are going to need luck, Wil."

"Can you tell me why?"

"It involves a test."

"Even homeschoolers don't take tests in the summer, Madame P.," Sonny said.

"Not that kind of test."

"What kind?" Wil asked.

"That part is cloudy." Madame Prévu shut her eyes, but opened them again almost immediately. "Wait!" Wil could see she was straining for words, or a thought, her eyes searching the air in front of her but not really looking at anything. She was thinking hard. Wil wanted to help her, like when Magnolia would supply a word for him that he couldn't come up with right away himself.

She reached into a pocket and pulled out a smooth pink stone. She put it in her left palm and traced circles with the fingers of her right hand. "There is an element I cannot reach."

Wil and Sonny exchanged a quick glance.

"It is something to do with watching." She held the pink stone to her temple and closed her eyes again briefly before shaking her head and slipping the stone back into her pocket. "You must watch carefully, Wil. That's all I can tell you now."

Wil nodded but had no idea how to respond to Madame Prévu's advice.

From her skirt pocket she now removed the beaded purse, from which she fished a few dollar bills. "Here—for the paper. You will come to see me again soon."

"Well, I'll be here tomorrow morning for sure, but you probably aren't up that early. . . ." The wind shifted suddenly, and a large set of glass chimes hanging from a tree in Madame Prévu's yard tinkled musically.

"I must meditate further to see if there is something more I can summon for you. I have the strong sense there is more you need to know, but for now: careful watching."

"Okay." Wil put a check mark in his ledger and stuffed the book in his back pocket. "Careful watching." He felt a little freaked out. "Got it."

"What the heck was that about?" Sonny said quietly as the two got on their bikes. Wil glanced back at the house. Madame Prévu was sitting cross-legged on her front porch with the backs of her hands resting on her knees and her eyes closed.

"Is there usually a lot of hocus-pocus with her?" Wil asked.

"Not really," Sonny said. "I mean, one time, back around sixth or seventh grade, she asked me what my sign was. I told her I guessed it was positive. I mean, I didn't even know then that people had signs, but I was pretty sure mine wasn't negative."

"I don't think that was a math question, Sonny."

"Well, I get it now but back then, we had just started doing operations with integers, and at first I thought that was some kind of surgery on your fingers. and I wondered what that possibly had to do with math, so what do I know?" Sonny coasted to a stop in front of the next customer's house. "But maybe if I had said negative, she would have poured the horseshoe over my head, too."

"Nothing's going to happen because she tipped that horseshoe over my head, Sonny," Wil said. But even as the words slipped out, he remembered the shivery feeling that washed over him on her porch, and doubt tugged at his thoughts. What did she mean by "careful watching"? Careful watching of what?

Fair Opens in Dweebville

Wil rested his chin on his hands in the open car window as they drove to the fair. The odd conversation with Madame Prévu haunted his thoughts. As advice, "careful watching" was pretty useless. What if he watched the wrong thing? Aw, shoot, he thought, glancing at the passing fields, searching for something without knowing what. It's just a bunch of hooey anyway. Madame Prévu seemed like a nice lady, but Wil didn't believe in any of that nonsense. Magic was just deception, sleight of hand. He knew there were people who took the newspaper just so they could follow their daily horoscope, but Wil didn't know what his own sign was. He did know enough to know it wasn't positive or negative.

"Can you roll that window up?" Trace interrupted Wil's thoughts. He held two tall paintings, framed in cardboard mats, upright on his lap. "The wind's blowing these things into my face."

"We'll die of the heat," Wil said, turning the crank.

"Pothole," Junior announced. Magnolia braced herself for the bump while Junior braked to a crawl. She was holding a cardboard flat with two dozen Maggie Pies.

"Sweet! A new ride!" Sonny pointed at the fairgrounds,

the top of which had come into view. A huge elliptical contraption with flashing lights towered above the tree line. Enclosed cars on a track did a figure eight as the long metal arm turned on its axis.

"That makes me feel green just looking at it," Magnolia said.

"We gotta drop off our entries first," Junior said, pulling into a parking space near the edge of a cornfield. "You boys want to pick a place to meet up at a particular time?"

From the parking lot, Wil could smell the funnel cakes frying. "You want us to wait for you to eat?"

"Heck, no," Junior said. He reached into his pocket and extracted two twenty-dollar bills. "Treat yourself to whatever you like."

Wil felt guilty taking the money. He knew he shouldn't, but he did. "Thanks, Dad."

"Why don't we all meet at eight at the far end of the midway?" Junior suggested.

"Pick me up at the main stage after you're through at the exhibition tent," Magnolia said, tucking her paperback into a canvas tote. "I'll sit in the back row."

"Won't it be noisy there, Mom?" Sonny asked.

"The cloggers are noisy, but I always feel bad that no one goes to those shows," she said. "At least I'm an audience. Oh, Wil—" She pulled a manila folder out of her bag. "Your essay. I had a copy in my office."

"My essay?"

"You know—'The History of Steele'? I checked and you're under the word limit. All I had to do was punch a hole in the top of it so they could display it if you win."

“If I win? Mom, I wasn’t planning on anybody ever reading that but you.”

“The winner gets a twenty-five-dollar gift card from the Village Booksmith in Coop de Ville.” she said.

Ooh. Wil loved the Village Booksmith. He put his hand out to take the essay.

“Tell you what,” she said. “I’ll turn it in for you. Go—have fun.”

Sonny and Wil followed the scent to the midway, lined with concession stands and prize booths. Wil got a hot dog with coleslaw—his favorite—but Sonny wanted to try something new.

“A deep-fried Twinkie?” Wil scrunched up his nose.

Sonny took a bite. White cream oozed from the cake, dripping onto the dusty ground. “Umpf. Iz gut.” He swallowed, then blew on the uneaten part. “Jeepers, that’s hot enough to nip the buds on my tongue. You want a bite?”

“I’ll pass,” Wil said. “Lookit that thing.” He pointed at a prize booth called the Looney Ladder. A pair of rope ladders were strung above an inflatable base. Two guys were racing each other to the top but kept falling off, thudding to the balloon below. A small crowd yelled out encouragement.

“How hard is it to climb a ladder?” Sonny asked.

“Probably harder than it looks,” Wil said.

“You wanna try? I’ll let you win.”

“Spend a dollar to win a twenty-five-cent toy? No thanks.” They kept walking.

"How about three balls in a bucket? Bet we could win, and it's a pretty big prize." Sonny pointed at a giant stuffed panda in a sealed plastic bag hanging from the rafters of the booth.

"Look at the bag, Sonny."

"Looks kinda cloudy, now that you mention it."

"That's dust. They've been carting these same stuffed animals from town to town for years 'cause nobody ever wins them. All of these games are fixed. The basketball is overinflated and the hoop is set at a different height than it usually is. The milk jugs you're supposed to knock down have weights in the bottom of them so it's almost impossible to tip them over. And even if you do win, the prizes are dumb. Why would I want a six-foot-tall SpongeBob?"

"Where did you see that?"

"I didn't see that, I'm just saying."

"Well, how about that underwater watch? It's still in the box."

"It probably doesn't work."

"They couldn't give it as a prize if it didn't work, could they?"

"It won't break till Monday, when the fair's gone. All this stuff is garbage, but they wouldn't get many people to play if they said, 'Step right up. Win some junk.'"

"But you know what they say, Wil. One man's junk is another man's garbage."

"You mean 'treasure.'"

"Exactly."

Wil shook his head. He should write down the things

Sonny said so he could enter them in the writing contest at next year's fair. If there was a humor category.

Sonny had turned his attention to another food stand. "That looks good, too. Want one?" He didn't wait for an answer.

Wil went to watch the target-shooting game while Sonny waited on line.

"This one's yours, kid." The carny patted one of the fake rifles that hadn't yet drawn a contestant. "We need one more player to start. Just two dollars. Wipe out the whole target and take your pick from the awesome prizes on the top row."

Wil had no intention of playing but he stepped forward, leaning down to peer through the sights of the gun. Just what he figured. It had an obvious tilt.

"Lemme see yours," he said to a younger kid standing at the next gun. The boy stepped aside.

"Your sight's tilted, too. If you try using it to hit the target, you'll spray to the left of it," Wil told him. "Just look at it with your eye."

"Thanks," the kid said.

The carny gave Wil a tight smile and gestured for him to come closer. Then he leaned over the counter and caught Wil by the collar of his T-shirt. Wil could smell cigarette smoke on the guy's breath as he whispered, forcefully, into Wil's ear, "Take a hike, buddy. You're messing in my kitchen."

Wil shook himself loose from the guy's grip just as Sonny joined him.

"What was that about?" Sonny said. "Here." He handed him a gooey, glistening black disk in a paper sleeve.

"What is that?"

"Deep-fried Oreo. Let's try that new ride. A guy on the Oreo line said it's five tickets but worth ten."

"As long as you sit in a different car. I don't want to be around when that Oreo makes a return appearance. Or the Twinkie."

"Ah, c'mon, Wil. You know I have an iron stomach. You don't want yours?"

Wil shook his head. They kept walking.

"You know what your problem is, Wil? You don't know how to live," Sonny told him between bites. They had walked almost the entire length of the midway and would have to stop to buy tickets for the rides. "If you never try anything new, you'll never know if it would've made you throw up or not."

Wil opened his mouth to point out the flaw in Sonny's logic, but Sonny cut him off. "Hey—look at that one. That's got to be rigged, huh?"

Wil followed the direction of Sonny's gaze and saw a crowd in front of the last booth on the midway. People were jostling for a spot to watch whatever was going on. A few men had kids on their shoulders; others were standing on tiptoe to see over the people in front. Wil's eyes drifted up to the banner above the booth:

Cover the Spot. Win $1,000 Grand Prize!

"If the underwater watches don't work, they're sure as snow in Alaska not giving away a thousand bucks, right?" Sonny said.

Wil remembered seeing this contest in the fair's advertisement in *The Caller.* "C'mon," he said, taking Sonny by the elbow and steering him away from the rides. "This is something I just might try."

Cover the Spot Game Reels in Contestants

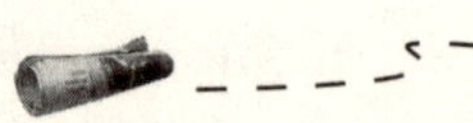

It took a few minutes and some assertive jostling, but Wil worked his way to the front. There was a small table, about ten feet from the counter, with a red circle in the middle of it about the size of a salad plate. Hanging from the rafters was a mirror, positioned so that even from the back of the crowd, the red circle was visible.

"Five dollars for a chance to win a grand!" the carny sang. Wil noticed the guy didn't need to do much advertising. The counter was lined with people, money in hand, waiting for a turn.

Sonny worked his way up to Wil's shoulder. "What's the catch?" he asked. Wil wanted to know the same thing. Both he and Sonny watched the man now playing. The carny had given him a blue disk, much smaller than the red circle on the table. Maybe the size of a saucer.

"You gotta completely cover the circle with those blue disks in three tries," Wil whispered.

The crowd "ooohed" when the man's first disk landed on the right side of the circle, covering about a third of it.

"Target hit!" the carny shouted. "Give him some room now, people. We may have a winner on our hands." He handed the contestant a second disk. The carny was a skinny guy, with a few days' growth of beard and close-cropped hair. His baggy carpenter's pants looked like they could use a wash. Even his nametag looked worn out. Wil could just make out that it read CARL, but the *a* was written in black marker while the rest of it was printed in blue. And it looked like something had been scratched out at the end.

The people around the contestant tried to inch back, like the carny requested, but the crowd wasn't budging. Was it possible to give away a thousand dollars every once in a while? Wil roughly calculated how many people were waiting to play, how many hours the fair was open, how much this game booth could take in at five dollars a pop. What if there were winners two days in a row, or three times in a weekend?

Or was there something crooked going on? The thought made Wil feel a little nauseous. It had taken him a few years, and probably twenty dollars of his own money, to figure out that the midway games were the least fun part of the fair. When he was younger, he had honestly thought there was a way of shooting out the entire target with a water pistol and winning a giant Big Bird. There had been heartbreak one summer when he finally won a goldfish in the ring-toss game, only to have the fish die on the way home. Wil learned the hard way that the games were skewed in favor of the carnies, and the prizes were not much to write home about. But surely the fair, *his fair*, the one held the same week as his birthday every year, wasn't involved in some kind of mass deception. Was it? Would they really deceive people into thinking somebody could win a thousand dollars if it wasn't possible? Wil didn't want to believe it, but the numbers just didn't add up.

The man threw his second disk. It fell beyond the circle, covering only a small crescent on the far end.

"A-w-w-w," the crowd groaned.

"Now, wait a second," the carny called. "Don't give up on him yet. He's got one more try. Let's everybody cheer him on."

The crowd applauded until the carny put his fingers to his lips and shushed them. Then he handed the man his last disk. "Good luck," the carny said, looking very serious.

A hush had fallen over the crowd, so Wil's voice was plainly heard when he snickered and mumbled, "Yeah, right." He regretted it immediately when the carny cast his eyes in Wil's direction.

The disk sailed, missing the red circle completely.

"It's harder than it looks," the contestant said, laughing off his defeat.

"Okay, who's next? Step right up. Five dollars to win a grand!"

Wil watched four more people lose—only one guy got even close—before Sonny tugged his arm. "If anybody could win this game, Wil, it's you."

Wil had been thinking the same thing. And a thousand dollars was more than enough for the laptop he wanted. "That spot's a lot smaller than a front porch," he said, considering.

"C'mon, then." Sonny pulled Wil's arm. "Let's try the new ride."

Wil left reluctantly. He had been trying to inch closer to the carny, who kept his stack of blue disks on the counter's ledge, under his left hand. Wil had a deep urge to swipe a disk. He wanted to feel the weight of it.

"You oughta play, Wil." Sonny said when they got free of the mob, back out onto the midway. "Nobody can nail a target better than you. Doc always said so."

Wil stopped and looked back at the booth. He agreed with Sonny. But he was also certain there was a catch, some trick that would prevent anybody from winning. What was it? From what he could see, the game looked pretty straightforward. "Look at that sign, Sonny—on the wall behind the table."

"You mean the one with the curvy girl?"

"No—the one to the left of that."

"I'd rather look at the curvy girl."

"That's what they're hoping. No—the one with the small print. Can you read that?"

Sonny squinted. "'Certain restrictions apply,'" he read. "'F. James Bates Family Fun Carnival, Inc., reserves the right to restrict participation . . .' I can't make out the rest from here."

"If I play, I don't want to come close. I want to win. And I think you gotta be ready to win the first time you play, or else."

"Or else what?"

"Or else maybe they come up with a way to make sure you don't get to play again."

Youth Breaches Fair Security

Friday morning Wil finished his route in forty minutes flat and kept pedaling, straining against gravity on the way up Wayout Hill. He'd left a note, saying not to wait for him for breakfast—he'd be home after the library.

Wil knew it was eight-point-six miles from the intersection of Wayin Road and Steele Highway to the Cooper County Fairgrounds, south of Dweebville. He wanted to be there as early as possible, hopefully before anybody else was awake.

The sun was high in the sky by the time he pushed his bike into a stand of trees at the near end of the fair property. He could see a chain-link fence he'd have to climb to get into the area where the rides were. The Cover the Spot booth, he remembered, was just beyond that. He decided it was more likely he'd run into someone in the parking lot, or along the midway, so chose to sneak in from the woods adjacent to the rides.

Scaling the fence was easy, although Wil was glad it wasn't topped with barbed wire, since he was wearing shorts and hadn't thought to bring gloves. Maybe that luck Madame Prévu spilled on his head was working, he thought, then chuckled. Wil put as much store in luck as he did in wishes.

The problem was how to get to the midway without getting noticed, since there was no one milling around. The rides looked asleep, their metal arms at rest, the swings stilled, the amplifiers that pumped out their music silent. Wil stood out just by being there. He hid behind one ride after another, making his way to the midway where . . . he saw another fence he'd have to climb. The rides themselves were cordoned off from the rest of the grounds. He had forgotten that, too. It was a shorter fence—not even as tall as Wil—but he'd be exposed for a second, sticking his head up high when he knew he should be keeping low. His palms had begun to sweat and not from the heat.

He hopped the second fence soundlessly by stepping on a ten-gallon bucket and bounding over in a single leap. Little puffs of dust erupted when he landed two-footed. He immediately ducked down and took a breath, trying to slow his racing heart.

A glance around revealed a deserted midway. The air smelled of rancid cooking oil, oil that should have been thrown out yesterday. Maybe the day before. He wondered if they'd change it before they started dunking Oreos and Twinkies into the fryers tonight. He was glad again that he didn't have Sonny's adventurous taste buds.

Wil took a deep breath and a quick glance around before striding quickly to the Cover the Spot booth. He ducked down again as soon as he reached it and waited until his heart slowed its hammering in his chest. There was no sound but a bird squawking as it flew by overhead. He steeled himself and made one more leap—over the counter of the booth.

In his pocket he had a piece of Trace's thin drawing paper. The red dot was really a circle of flexible plastic—like a giant rubber jar opener. It was affixed to the top of a square table. A cloth stapled around all four sides of the table fell to the dirt floor of the booth. Wil lifted the cloth to see if there was anything underneath it: just the table's legs. He pulled the paper and a pencil from his pockets and quickly made a tracing of its circumference. He'd measure it later. Up close it was larger than Wil had figured—closer to the size of a dinner plate.

He heard a dog bark and dropped to a squat. There were shelves beneath the counter, and affixed to one, a metal box with a red button on the front and wires coming out the back. It looked like some kind of alarm signal. Wil pushed a roll of paper towels aside and opened the one cardboard box he found, but he didn't see the blue disks. Dang! They had to be around here somewhere. He was about to lift the tablecloth to see if they were stored under it when he heard a shout.

"Hey, Wyatt! How'd it go last night?"

He scrambled under the table.

"Pretty quiet. Just a couple drunks we had to show the door."

"Nothing like the brouhaha in Satellite City, huh?"

A "brouhaha"? Wil puzzled over the word as he heard feet shuffling past the booth and the *clank, clank* sound of a chain.

"That was a close call for ole Jimbo. How he wiggled out of that one, I'm still not sure. . . ."

Wil strained to hear the rest of the conversation but the voices grew fainter, the clanking noise just a tinkling in the distance.

He lifted the tablecloth and crawled over to the counter, lifting himself up just enough to peek out. He saw a security guard unlocking the gate to the ride area. The guard had a German shepherd on a leash. There was another guy in a baseball cap, carrying a go cup. Just as Wil was about to duck again, he caught sight of the dog—looking directly at him.

Wil scooted back under the table as quick as he could. Too late. The dog barked ferociously.

He heard the feet again, running now. The security guard shouted, "Steady, Jake."

Wil pulled himself into the tightest curl possible, his arms wrapped around his legs. He tried not to breathe. He wondered how he could stop himself from giving off a scent, because surely the dog would smell him.

He heard the snuffling of the dog's nose on the other side of the booth. The guard was silent. Wil could almost feel the dog's hot breath—he was that close. He wondered if the dog would bite him, how bad it would hurt . . .

"You knothead, Jake," the guard said, laughing. "You had me there."

"What's he got?" came the other voice.

"Leave it, Jake. NOW!" the guard commanded. "Half-eaten pretzel. This dog'd sell you out to anybody for a day-old corn fritter."

Wil heard the old guy grunt, then the metal squeak of

a trash-can lid swinging open and the *thunk* of something falling in.

He didn't allow himself to exhale until the footsteps faded again. He thought back to the luck Madame Prévu had poured over his head, not dismissing it this time. Maybe she had been right. Maybe he did need it.

Web Search Turns Up Tantalizing Tidbit

The lock on the metal box wouldn't budge. The box itself was bolted to the shelf, so Wil couldn't even shake it to see if the blue disks were inside. He had no choice but to leave, sneaking out the way he'd snuck in. No way was he going to risk running into Jake again. He had a feeling this dog's bite was worse than his bark. And the bark had nearly scared Wil's skin off.

The guard had left the gate to the ride area unlocked. Wil walked briskly but casually through it, pretending he belonged there. He didn't even turn around when he hopped the second fence. A hundred yards inside the stand of trees, he stopped and let out a deep breath. He pulled the paper with the circle on it from his back pocket to make sure he still had it. He had only accomplished half of what he'd set out to do, but the hard part was done. For sure, though, he had to get back to the fair tonight. How was he going to do that? Junior and Trace wouldn't want to come back until Sunday, when the prize ribbons would be awarded.

He swung his leg over his bike, his head filled with thoughts. In no time, he was coasting down Wayout Hill, passing the turnoff to his own street. He needed to stop at the library.

There were a few people already waiting for their turn at the computers when Wil got there, but it was wonderfully cool in the building, so he was more than willing to wait. He put his name on the sign-up sheet and went to read the newspapers.

He took *The Caller* and *The Satellite Valley News* from the shelf and plunked down in a soft chair. His legs felt like overcooked spaghetti after cycling something close to twenty-five miles that morning. A wave of sleepiness hit until the photo on *The Caller*'s front page—two kids on the new ride at the fair screaming like their hair was on fire—shook him awake. He had to admit the new ride, the Wild Snake, was wicked good.

He read through both papers before he heard Ms. Parsons call his name in a loud whisper, letting him know it was his turn. He quickly folded the newspapers and returned them to the shelf.

He had an e-mail waiting! 'Bout time that jerky Double-G sent me an answer, he thought, clicking on the Read icon. But it wasn't from Dweeb. It was from Fleur.

To: WilofSteele@topmail.net

From: FleursAbroad@sudamerinet.com

Subj: Been thinking

Wrote a letter to the editor of The Satellite Valley News about The Caller and you should, too. You gotta fight this thing. Why, this reminds me of the time in France I joined a protest against irregular meat. We flung organic tomatoes at a grocer who was selling that stuff 'til he came out and pleaded with us to stop. "Sock Ray Blue," he said, which is French for "goodness gracious." (Them French got some funny expressions.) But I bet he never sold a cellophane packet of nuked ground beef again. He's probably a vegan, we had him so shook up.

The point is, Wil, they're expecting you to fold like an ironing board 'cause they think they're dealing with a kid. YOU'RE NO KID, Wil! You're a David. A member of the newspaper-carrying line of Davids that stretches back nearly to the dawn of the twentieth century! They can't just stop bringing news to Steele because they want more profit. They make plenty of money from those grocery inserts.

¿What's your plan, Wil? Keep me in the loop.

Love,
Fleur

P.S. ¿Print out the letter for me, will ya, and have Maggie look it over before you mail it? Not sure I spelled weezil right—weezil as in those nasty sneaky no-good rotten critters that were always stealing eggs when Doc kept

```
chickens. Smelt bad, too. Not Doc, I mean.
The weezils.
```

Wil looked around to see if anybody else was waiting for the computer. Fleur's mention of writing to *The Satellite Valley News* reminded him of what the guy with the go cup had said earlier—about the "brouhaha" at the fair during its stop in Satellite City. Would it have been reported in the paper? What was a "brouhaha" anyway? He thought he knew—some sort of fuss.

He typed in the URL for his favorite online dictionary, then "brouhaha" in the search box:

> **brou·ha·ha (bro͞o′hä hä′, bro͞o hä′ hä)** n. [Fr; orig. *brru, ha, ha!*; in medieval theater, cry of devil disguised as clergy:] a noisy stir or wrangle; hubbub; uproar; commotion.

Uproar. Commotion. Wil dashed to the reading area to retrieve the paper he'd just read, opening it to page 2, where there was a listing of the newspaper's address and the names of the people who edited different sections. Yes! They also had an online edition. He rushed back to the computer and pecked in the URL.

The home page came up. Wil scrolled through until he found "Archives."

He typed in "Satellite Valley Fair" and "brouhaha."

The hourglass appeared on his screen as the computer did its work.

The screen pulsed.

Your search did not match any articles:

- Make sure words are spelled correctly.
- Try different words.
- Try more general words.
- Visit the **Search Help** page for assistance.

Okay, so nobody else called whatever uproar had happened a "brouhaha." He deleted "brouhaha" and left "Satellite Valley Fair." A hit!

Article 1 of 462; 817 words

Ugh. Four hundred and sixty-two articles? He didn't have enough time left to start scrolling through all of them. What the heck. There's only one kind of brouhaha that really interests me, Wil thought as he typed in "Cover the Spot game" next to "Satellite Valley Fair."

He held his breath while the computer worked.

Bingo.

Article 1 of 3; 723 words

Published on June 28, Page 1A, *Satellite Valley News, The* (PA)

Fair Owner Denies Wrongdoing; Carnival Worker Fired

By Phoebe Flowers, Staff Writer

(Satellite City, June 27) F. James "Jimbo" Bates, president of Bates Family Fun Carnival, announced at a news conference Monday that he had terminated the employee responsible for the alleged rigging of the Cover the Spot game at this year's Livingston County Fair.

Bates spoke from the platform of the caboose on his 62-car train, moments before it pulled out of Satellite Valley Station, bound for the next stop on the fair's 18-city summer tour.

"I am aghast and appalled that anyone would sully the good name of my family's business with such shenanigans," said Bates, who said he fired Frances "Curly" Moffitt, the worker accused . . .

Note: Searching the archives of *The Satellite Valley News* is always free! The first 100 words of any article are free for 30 days after publication. There is a $2.95 fee to view the full text of any article. Credit cards or PayPal accepted. Open an account and receive your first 10 articles free with secured deposit!

Article 2 of 3; 654 words

Published on June 26, Page 1B, *Satellite Valley News, The* (PA)

‹ satellite valley news exclusive ›

Fairgoer Alleges Fraud at Midway Carnival Game; S.V. Police Investigating

By Phoebe Flowers, STAFF WRITER

(Satellite City, June 25) A Florida man has asked the Livingston County Sheriff's Department to investigate the alleged rigging of a carnival game at this year's Satellite Valley Fair.

Wade Hodson, 28, went to police after dozens of witnesses say he won the fair's Cover the Spot game Friday night.

"I won fair and square, and there were plenty of witnesses not even related to me who will testify to that," said Hodson, a NASA aerospace engineer in town visiting his wife's family.

Hodson says he had fulfilled the requirements of the game (see diagram, p. 7B) and was owed the game's $1,000 prize until the carnival worker in charge . . .

Note: Searching the archives of *The Satellite Valley News* is always free! The first 100 words of any article are free for 30 days after publication. There is a $2.95 fee to view the full text of any article. Credit cards or PayPal accepted. Open an account and receive your first 10 articles free with secured deposit!

Article 3 of 3; 781 words

Published on June 23, Page 1E, *Satellite Valley News, The* (PA)

Fair to Open Featuring Cheap Thrills and Lucrative Prizes

By Phoebe Flowers, STAFF WRITER

(Satellite City, June 22) The 89th Annual Satellite Valley Fair opens tonight with new amusement rides, tasty foods, live pig races, a bake-off contest, and games of skill, including one that carries a grand prize of $1,000.

"Bates Family Fun has been the number-one provider of touring, wholesome entertainment in the South Central Downstate region for nearly 90 years," said F. James "Jimbo" Bates, company president. "This year, we're also planning to make a few people rich with our new Cover the Spot game."

The game looks easy enough, but as this reporter can attest, you'll have to have mighty good aim to go home with more money than you brought!

Note: Searching the archives of *The Satellite Valley News* is always free! The first 100 words of any article are free for 30 days after publication. There is a $2.95 fee to view the full text of any article. Credit cards or PayPal accepted. Open an account and receive your first 10 articles free with secured deposit!

Steele Boy Opens Investigation

"Whatcha reading, Wil?"

Wil had been so absorbed in the newspaper stories about the Satellite Valley Fair that it took him a second to register Ann-Douglas sliding into the chair beside him. Now she was peering at his computer. He minimized the screen quickly. "Nothing," he said.

"Gosh. Top secret, huh? These are *public* computers, Wil," she said, turning back to her own screen.

Now he'd offended her. "No, sorry, I was reading some newspaper stories. You just startled me."

"Did you get your problem with the newspaper route settled?"

How did she know he had a problem with his newspaper route? "What problem?"

"I don't know. Whatever problem it was that you had Sonny help you with. Your mother told me."

"Oh." She didn't really know anything. She just hung around his house enough to know something was up. Wil wished Ann-Douglas had brothers or sisters of her own, or more friends. He'd seen less of her before Olivia, her best friend, had moved somewhere east when her father had found a job there. Both Ann-Douglas's parents worked in Dweebville, so he guessed she was lonely at home, but why did she have to constantly intrude on his life? "No, I didn't."

"Wanna see the photos I'm thinking of entering in the fair?" she asked. "Your mother helped me come up with a great title for this series, and I had them burned to a disk, so if the judges want they can take them home and review them. And I'm going to put a little music underneath it, too. Make a montage."

"You can do all that on the library's computer?" Wil asked.

"Oh, I have software my parents bought me as a present for making the all-A honor roll," she said.

"So why are you here?"

"To download the song I want. The connection here is much faster than at home. It would tie up the phone line for hours, and my parents don't want the phone busy while they're at work, because even though they gave me a cell phone, the only time I can get a signal is when I'm at school."

Ann-Douglas had her own cell phone? Who would she call? Jealousy was not an emotion Wil felt very often, but he felt a pang of it thinking about Ann-Douglas with her own computer and her special software and her cell phone that she barely had any use for. "I gotta go, Ann-Douglas," he said, and he did. He needed to find the full text of the articles about the Cover the Spot game from a month-old *Satellite Valley News*. He knew it wouldn't be on the shelf. It seemed like they never kept more than a week's worth. What exactly was the carny accused of doing? he wondered. Because even if that worker had been fired, Wil needed to know if the new guy running the game was doing the same thing before Wil himself tried playing.

His first idea was to contact the man mentioned in one of the articles—Wade Hodson. Had Hodson actually gotten the money? He wanted to talk to him, but the details in the article—"a Florida man," "visiting his wife's family"—wouldn't help Wil track down somebody who had visited Satellite Valley weeks ago. The guy was probably back home already. Even calling directory assistance wouldn't help, because Wil didn't know where in Florida Hodson lived. So he Googled the man's name, typing in "aerospace engineer" and "Florida," and got a huge number of hits—but they were all scientific papers, and notices of presentations Mr. Hodson was supposed to give, and awards his team at NASA had received for a study on the "ballistic entry trajectory of spacecraft reentering Earth's atmosphere." Wow, this Hodson guy really *is* a rocket scientist, Wil thought. But none of the information included a phone number, or even the name of the city where he lived.

Wil logged off the computer and headed to Ms. Parsons's desk. She picked up her clipboard when she saw him coming.

"Can you find Grace Prillaman and tell her it's her turn?" she asked. "I saw her headed toward the music CDs."

"Sure, Ms. Parsons, but can I ask you something?" He waited till she nodded. "Is there a way to get the full article from an old copy of *The Satellite Valley News*? I can only get the first hundred words online without paying." If anybody could figure out how to get him a copy, it'd be Ms. Parsons. She was the one who had found the Future Physicists of America Listserv for him a few years back.

"We don't have access to it ourselves, Wil," she said after clicking through a few databases on her computer. "How soon do you need it?"

"Um. As soon as possible?"

"Well, I can put in a request to open an account with them—for the future—but I'll also call over to the Livingston County Library. Maybe they've got a copy and we can request an interlibrary loan. We don't normally do that with periodicals, but . . . Write down the dates of the issues you need."

Wil took the scrap paper and pencil she handed him and scribbled down the dates of the newspaper articles he wanted. "When should I check back?"

"You'll be in tomorrow, right?"

He nodded.

"I'll try to come up with something for you by then."

"Thanks, Ms. Parsons." Wil wasn't the demonstrative type, but he had to suppress an urge to hug her.

Getting on his bike, he realized his next mission would be figuring out a way to get back to the fair tonight. He had to watch the Cover the Spot game—and the carny—even more closely, without being watched himself.

Meantime, he was starved.

Cooper County Memorial Library ✻ Steele Branch

95 Mane Street, Steele, PA 16028

To: *Mary Pressick, Cooper County Memorial Library Chief*

From: *Jami Parsons, Steele Branch, Head Librarian*

Date: *July 29*

Re: *Newspaper databases*

I have had a request from a patron that we open a subscription account with The Satellite Valley News *archives department. He was interested in reading the full text of an article that he found an abstract of online, but there was, of course, a charge. As you know,* The News *is not one of the newspapers available through our integrated data source—none of our regional newspapers are—so the full text is not available to us that way.*

Because this patron was very eager to find this one particular article, I did search the recyclables, but that week's papers had been picked up already. Is it perhaps time to rethink our policy of outprocessing hard copies after only seven days? I know there are shelving issues, but the article in question was around a month old and already unavailable to us. I contacted Annabelle Hoffman (she said to say hello!) at the Satellite Valley branch of the Livingston County Library. She was able to find the article in question and is mailing me a copy (their fax is down—technology!), but surely we can do better for our patrons.

Please advise on the account issue.

Collision Results in Lucky Run-in

"Lookie who's here," Junior called when Wil came in the back door. "We were just about to divide up your stuff."

"You set a new record, Wil," Trace said. The Davids were all sitting around the kitchen table eating grilled cheese on focaccia. Junior made a mean focaccia, with fresh rosemary from the garden and olive oil from a huge tin can Fleur had brought home from Greece, where she had worked on a project to protect endangered sponge populations.

"What record?"

"*Longest* amount of time it ever took to do the route," Trace mumbled. His mouth was full.

"You get lost?" Sonny asked.

That question didn't deserve an answer, Wil thought, except that Sonny had asked it. "Didn't you see my note? I said I was going to the library right after I was done."

"But the library doesn't open till nine," Magnolia cut in. "Did you have something to read?"

"I was thinking."

"Uh-oh," Magnolia and Junior said together. Wil thinking often led to some big, new labor-intensive project that could consume not only his complete attention but command the assistance of several other family members as well.

"Sandwich?" Junior offered Wil the plate. Wil took one.

"Anybody want to go to the fair tonight?" Wil asked.

"You come into some money?" Trace helped himself to another sandwich.

"That first week's worth of tips is burning a hole in your pocket, isn't it, Wil?" Junior said. "I remember that feeling. Like you had to spend it even if there wasn't anything you really wanted to buy."

"So you'll go?" Wil brightened at how easily he had gotten what we wanted.

"Ah, no, Wil. But if you want to spend your tips, you can chip in toward the seed money we need to get the county to look for a tenant for the hairpin factory."

Magnolia laughed, but not joyfully. More like a snort. Wil was confused. "What does that mean?"

"Your daddy is being sarcastic, Wil," Magnolia said. "He had his meeting with the Economic Development Council this morning."

Wil had forgotten all about it. "What's 'seed money'?"

"Seed money is usually some modest amount of money contributed to get a project going, or to attract additional financing," Magnolia said. "It's a form of venture capitalism."

"The county wants the town to put up some of its own funds that they'll match with tax dollars," Junior continued. "Then they'll offer that pot of money to a business as an incentive to get them to relocate to the hairpin factory."

"How much do they need?" Trace asked.

"They'll match whatever we can raise, but the figures they're talking about are in the thousands-of-dollars range."

"Oh," Wil said.

"Hasn't anybody told them that when people are out of work they don't have money to give away, never mind buy seeds?" Sonny asked.

Junior paused to consider how to answer Sonny's question. Then he shook his head to clear it. "Let me explain it another way, son. They want to see that a community is serious about supporting a local business before they sink *their* money and time into finding a tenant. There are people out of work in other towns, too, and there are other vacant buildings." He scrunched his napkin up and put it on his plate. "It's probably easier to see the logic of it if when it's happening to somebody else."

The table was quiet, not even the scratch of a fork. Wil's parents never discussed their finances in front of the kids. But since Junior's unemployment checks had run out, Wil knew his dad had been driving to other towns, filling out applications. Wil had overheard his mother on the telephone telling someone that Junior had to take a job, even if it was a bad one, so the family would have health insurance. Wil hated the thought of his father having to leave Steele every day to do a job he didn't like. He had planned to chip in money for groceries or whatever as soon as he got the laptop. It was probably selfish to think about getting a computer at all when his parents were taking money from their savings to buy food, but he had been able to push that thought away whenever it tried crowding out his laptop wish. His parents were always insisting the money from the route belonged to the boys. They'd probably refuse Wil's offer. "Is there any way the town could raise the seed money?" Wil asked.

"The Town Council's meeting Monday night. I'll go and give an update, and we'll see if anybody has any good ideas. But the town's suffering, too. The hairpin factory was the biggest taxpayer by far in Steele. Just 'cause it closed doesn't mean the roads don't still need to be paved and the light bills paid. They're trying to get by with less, too."

No one had anything to say to that. After a pause that went on a moment too long to be comfortable, Magnolia said, "I'll do the dishes."

"I'll do 'em, Mom," Sonny offered, collecting plates.

"But we'll go to the fair tomorrow, Wil," Junior said, clapping Wil gently on the back. "See if one of us picked up a ribbon."

"Okay, Dad," Wil said. "It's no big deal."

"I didn't mean to worry anybody," Junior said, handing his plate to Sonny. "We're gonna be just fine. The house is paid off, we got a garden, we got neighbors who bring us blueberries, and we got each other. "

"And we have books to read," Magnolia said, with a smile at Junior. She put her arm around his shoulder, and he leaned in to kiss her on the cheek.

After lunch, Sonny found Wil lying on the front lawn. "You still thinking?"

"Yeah," Wil said.

“Hope that’s not contagious.” He plopped onto the grass next to Wil. “It’s summer, y’know.”

“If ever there was a bad time to lose the newspaper route, it’s now,” Wil said.

“It does seem like that, doesn’t it,” Sonny said.

“Fifty dollars a week would go a long way in our house.”

“Junior has never let me give him any money, though. I’ve offered,” Sonny said.

“So you must have some saved, right?” A fast-moving white cloud scudded by, momentarily blocking out the sun.

“I’m got some put away for when we run out of pears, sure,” he said.

“You want to help me finish collecting today?”

“Yeah, but wait a few hours. Late afternoon, people’ve been to the bank.”

“I guess we’re lucky anybody still takes the paper at all with so many people out of work,” Wil said.

Sonny stretched out alongside his brother. “They need the paper to look for jobs in the classifieds, that’s what Junior says. That cloud looks like Mrs. Spanko, don’t it, Wil? Remember? My second-grade teacher? The one with the buckteeth and the big hair that looked like it was cemented in place?”

They could look for jobs online if they had laptops, Wil thought, but he suddenly felt too tired to get the words out. All that cycling . . .

“Only Mrs. Spanko was taller than that cloud,” Sonny said. “That cloud looks like a shorter, fatter version of Mrs. Spanko, but the hair and the teeth . . . don’t you see it, Wil?”

No response. Sonny rolled onto his side and propped himself up. "Well, I'll be a monkey's uncle. When's the last time *you* took an afternoon nap?"

Wil had fallen fast asleep.

Magnolia planted an umbrella over her youngest son so the sun wouldn't broil his skin to a ruby crisp. Wil slept the exhausted sleep of the nearly dead for two hours. When he woke, he was groggy and sweaty and there were, in fact, ants in his pants.

"I always thought that was just an expression," he said as he put the ants onto the windowsill before taking a shower.

Sonny had the bikes out and was waiting for him by the time he'd dressed. "How many we get yesterday?" he asked.

"Sixty-three, which is seventy-two percent. Is that pretty typical?"

"Well, you're the math whiz, but I think the percentages stay the same every time you do 'em."

"No, I mean, is that about the same rate as every week—about seventy percent on Thursday?"

"Heck, Wil, like I told you, I take math off for the summer," Sonny said. "But we'll get another twenty or so today, I bet. Then we'll have to go to the last four or five every day till next Thursday to get the rest."

Sonny was basically right. But today most of the people they hadn't collected from were *waiting* for them when they arrived.

"You bring that petition?" Mrs. Blanchard asked.

"I want to sign that list you've got going around—about the newspaper?" Mr. Roberts demanded.

"Is it true what Señor Lopez Lopez told me?" Mrs. Pulliam asked. "The newspaper is cutting us out of the loop?"

Wil and Sonny told the story a dozen times, gathering a signature or two or three at every stop, while assuring their customers they were going to fight *The Caller*'s decision.

"Just because we're small and remote doesn't mean we're backward," Mr. Anderson told them.

So cheered was Wil by the reaction of his neighbors—their indignation, their fighting spirit—that he very nearly forgot about the fair. He very nearly forgot how important it was he get there that night if he was going to figure out how the Cover the Spot game was rigged. He did forget, completely, that he was riding a bike down a hill till he saw—too late—Judge Salzberg backing out of her driveway.

"Wil! Look out!" Sonny called, but Wil had already hit the brakes hard, screeching to a halt. To keep himself from flying over the handlebars, he leaped from the bike as it skidded sideways, the front tire thudding hard into the passenger-side door of Judge Salzberg's station wagon.

He caught a glimpse of Ann-Douglas's horror-stricken face in the backseat as he flew off his bike. Judge Salzberg quickly put the car in park and opened her door.

"Judge Salzberg, I'm so sorry! There's no dent or anything," Wil stammered.

"My word, Wil, who cares about the wagon? Are you all right?"

"Fine. I'm fine." He looked down mournfully at his bike. "But I did a number on my front wheel." The tube had come off when the rim bent. "I wasn't watching where I was going."

"That was scary. I thought you were going to crash right into *me*," Ann-Douglas said. "Didn't it look like that, Sonny?"

Wil stood the bike up, assessing the damage. He had never wiped out on his bike before.

"You able to ride that bike home, Wil?" Judge Salzberg asked.

"No, I'll have to walk it." And use Sonny's bike in the morning.

"Put it in the back of the wagon and I'll run you home. I'm going past your place anyway. You get any more signatures on that petition?" she asked.

"Judge Salzberg and I called everybody in her address book!" Ann-Douglas said.

"Yes, ma'am, we sure did. People told us you'd called them about it," Sonny said, lifting the hatch of Judge Salzberg's station wagon while Wil turned the bike sideways to wedge it into the back. It wouldn't fit all the way in, but there was a short rope in a cargo net that he used to tie the hatch down partway.

"Thanks, Judge Salzberg," Wil said. "I'm really sorry about that. My mind was somewhere else."

"I'm just happy you aren't hurt, Wil," she said. "Hop in now. I've got to be at the fair by six."

Investigator Returns to Scene of the Crime

Judge Salzberg had to be the slowest driver in Cooper County, Wil thought. She crept through intersections even when there was no stop sign.

"You have that petition with you?" she asked. She was taking long slugs of something from one of those insulated go cups. Wil thought it an odd time of day to be drinking coffee.

"Right here," he said, pulling the petition from his back pocket.

"Hold my milk, please," she said, handing the cup to Sonny. There had been a kerfuffle at Wil's house when Ann-Douglas tried to insist that Sonny sit in the back-seat with her. Judge Salzberg did not allow riders in the front seat who did not yet weigh a hundred pounds. Wil weighed only ninety-four, which wasn't much but was six or seven pounds more than Ann-Douglas.

"Milk?" Sonny asked.

"I always drink half a pint and take two antacids before this event." Judge Salzberg was on her way to the fair to pick a winner in the chili cook-off. "Coats my stomach so all that spice doesn't burn a hole in it."

"Good idea," Sonny said. Wil guessed Sonny was thinking about how this method might help him prepare for his own next meal at the fair. Sonny hadn't slept well the night before—tossing, turning, moaning—as his deep-fried dinner worked its way through his plumbing.

Judge Salzberg had one eye on the road and one scanning the petition. "Looks like you got near everybody in Steele already, Wil!"

"We let any kid who could write his name sign, so we got more than two hundred signatures."

"Time to widen the net."

"Is this about the Internet, too?" Sonny asked.

"No, I mean catch more fish."

Sonny laughed. "Oh, I get it. Catch fish with the Inter*net*. Funny."

Judge Salzberg cast a glance at Wil in the rearview mirror. "I mean you ought to circulate it at the fair. Steele folks haven't got a monopoly on what's right and reasonable. You tell people from other towns about it—people *The Caller* will still be counting on to take the paper—I think your petition will pack more punch."

Wil could see she was right. "I'll do that. I'm not much of a chili eater anyway, if you don't mind."

"Got any more of that milk?" Sonny asked. "I *am* a chili eater."

"Get the antacids from the glove box, Sonny. We'll get you a pint before we start."

Wil turned to Ann-Douglas, who was scrunched against the passenger-side door, apparently trying to sit as far away from him as she possibly could. "Are you a chili eater?"

he asked. Wil figured she would stick close to whatever Sonny was doing but wanted to make sure she wasn't going to follow him around.

"Only if it's vegetarian," she said. "I should've entered my Three Bean TVP chili. It's delicious *and* it's healthy."

"TVP?" Wil wondered.

"Aha! Something Einstein doesn't know?" Ann-Douglas.

"Television program?" Sonny guessed.

"Textured Vegetable Protein," she said. Wil thought he heard a touch of smugness in her reply.

Wil wondered about the "texture" part of that ingredient but decided to look it up online rather than risk a lecture. "Texture" sounded like cardboard. He made a mental note to not eat anything Ann-Douglas ever offered him. For somebody so skinny, she sure seemed to spend a lot of time in the kitchen.

"I'm going to check out the competition in the photography tent," she said, announcing her agenda for the evening.

He left all three of them in the exhibition area, saying he'd collect some signatures on the midway. He needed Sonny's help for what he really came to do, but he could do a little surveillance on his own first.

"I want to ride that new whipsaw-thingy—the Wild Snake," Judge Salzberg said before they parted ways. "Let us get our business done here, and I'll treat. If we like it, we'll do it twice."

Wil nodded, wondering if Sonny had another night of agitated groaning in store after chili sampling and a couple of turns on the Snake. There was no point mentioning this.

He'd learned a long time ago there was no possibility of talking sense into Sonny, especially if fun was involved.

He made his way to the Cover the Spot game without bothering to ask for anybody's signature. He needed Sonny for that, too. One of his brother's talents—although Wil wasn't sure that was the right word—was that he wasn't a bit shy about approaching strangers. It was like he didn't even know it wasn't done. Once, at a video store, Wil had seen Sonny, without a lick of embarrassment, strike up a conversation with a cardboard cutout of Buzz Lightyear.

Another big crowd had gathered in front of the Cover the Spot booth. That one thousand dollar prize was irresistible, Wil thought. Wil pulled his Pirates cap down low over his eyes and went around the side so he'd be standing where the carny would have his back to him. He wished he'd measured the distance between where the player stood to throw and where the spot was when he'd been there that morning, but he hadn't thought of it then. And he had risked becoming dog chow if he'd hung around any longer. He wondered where Jake the Trash-Eating Watchdog was now. Probably having his teeth sharpened.

He also wished he could secretly take a photograph of the booth—several actually, from different angles—so he could study them at home. One contestant landed the first two disks on the spot, and Wil noticed the carny moved closer to the table before he gave him the third disk. It sailed wide of the target and didn't cover any part of the spot at all. Wil watched for more than an hour before Sonny startled him by tapping him on the shoulder.

"You ready?" Sonny put his hand to his mouth to cover

a loud burp. "Man, some of that chili could take paint off a car."

"You pick a winner?"

"Judge S. did. There was one batch that actually made steam come out of our ears. You ready to ride the Snake?"

"If you are," Wil said.

There was a line, but when they got to the front of it, Judge Salzberg insisted on letting people behind them pass so they could ride in the first car. "Get our money's worth," she said.

At Wil's prompting, Sonny used the time to get everybody in line to sign the petition.

"You do the talking," Wil said. "I'll get the signatures."

Judge Salzberg and Ann-Douglas turned out to be the kind of people who raise their arms over their heads and belt out screams for the entire length of a ride. "Pretty good," Judge Salzberg said as the car rolled to a stop. "Wanna do it again?"

"I will!" Ann-Douglas said.

Sonny looked wobbly and pale. "I'll pass," he said weakly.

"Me, too," Wil added. "We can collect some more signatures if you want to, though."

"Are you sure, Sonny?" Ann-Douglas said. "You could sit with me in the second car and we could let Judge Salzberg have the front all to herself."

"I'm sure," he said woozily.

"You don't mind waiting?" Judge Salzberg asked.

"Heck, no, Judge S. We wouldn't have even gotten here tonight if I hadn't crashed into your car."

"Deal, then. Where you boys gonna be?"

"How 'bout we meet you at the entrance to the ride area?" Wil said.

"Perfect," she responded. "C'mon, Ann. We're good for another go, right?" She put her arm around the girl's narrow shoulders. Ann-Douglas slipped her arm around Judge Salzberg's waist. Everybody loved Ann-Douglas. Why did she annoy Wil so much? He watched them until they rejoined the line. By the time he turned back to his brother, Sonny had recovered from his dizziness and corralled four girls, all of them wearing itty-bitty shorts and bathing suit tops.

"Wil, these ladies would love to sign our petition. Name and phone number, please."

Wil handed the petition and a pen to a blonde in a polka-dot top with only enough fabric for about six dots. Sonny bent in half so she could lean on his back to sign.

The blonde's redheaded friend peered closely at the paper. "Hey, none of these other people gave you their phone numbers."

Sonny twisted his head around, his own blond hair falling across his eyes. "None of them were as pretty as you."

The girls giggled. Wil groaned. What happens to boys' brains when they turn fourteen? he wondered. How can I prevent it from happening to mine?

After each of the girls took her turn scribbling across Sonny's back, he thanked them, flashing a smile that revealed his one dimple. They moved away in a tight clump, talking all at once.

"Shucks, this is like catching fish in a bathtub," Sonny

said, watching another set of girls sashay hip-to-hip down the midway. "Look—there's another bunch who I am sure would like to help us out."

"Hang on, lover boy." Wil put the brakes on by grabbing Sonny's arm. "We got one other thing to do before we leave." He took a five-dollar bill from his pocket and gave it to Sonny. "I need you to play the Cover the Spot game."

"Me? Wil, you should do it. Just close your eyes and pretend that red spot has the words *Dobro došli* written on it and you're there."

"I don't want you to win, Sonny."

"You don't?"

Wil cut his eyes toward the crowd at the booth, then pulled Sonny close and whispered instructions in his ear.

"Huh. You gonna tell me *why* I'm doing this?"

"Yes. Later."

"It's your money."

Sonny worked his way to the front and handed his money to the carny. Following Wil's instructions, he was careful not to even look to his right—toward the side of the booth where Wil told him he'd be standing.

His first throw landed just to the left of the spot's center. The second covered the bottom third. A current of something like electricity quickly surged through the crowd.

The carny, Wil noticed, moved closer to the table.

Wil looked at the spot in the mirror suspended from the booth's ceiling. Would a perfect throw cover the rest of the spot? He couldn't be sure from this distance. The curve of circle that was exposed might be larger than the diameter of the remaining disk.

In the mirror, Wil noticed something else. The carny moved away from the table. It seemed like he had reached under the counter for something. Wil couldn't see what, but the carny was standing near the area where Wil had seen the metal box that morning. The one that looked like it had some sort of alarm button.

The crowd got louder. The carny seemed to be stalling, talking up how close Sonny had come with the first two disks, letting the tension build. Was he deliberately trying to make Sonny nervous?

Or was he waiting for something else? Was he waiting for someone he'd summoned with the alarm button to arrive?

Finally, the carny handed over the third disk. Sonny didn't hesitate. He flicked his wrist sharply and the disk spun wildly, behind the carny's back and off to the side, toward the fence that separated the rides from the midway.

Wil casually sauntered to the spot where the disk had landed and picked it up.

"Hey, kid! Toss that back here!" the carny called.

But Wil kept walking, the third disk safely tucked away in his pocket.

Smashing Investigation Yields No New Clues 

Wil headed to his bedroom, Sonny on his heels. He slid open the top drawer of the desk he shared with his brothers, where he'd hidden the tracing he'd made of the spot. He removed it, and one of his brother's art tablets, and laid them on the desk.

"Y'know, if you hadn't made me throw that to you, I might be a thousand dollars richer right now," Sonny said. "My first two throws covered most of the spot."

"I doubt it," Wil said. With a pencil he outlined the circumference of the disk on a sheet from Trace's tablet.

"Yeah, it would've been tough," Sonny admitted. "I had a little showing at the top and part of the left, but if I could've slid the third one so it knocked the disk at the bottom to the left a bit . . ."

Wil stacked a couple sheets of paper neatly so he could cut two circles at once. "C'mere," he said to Sonny, putting down the scissors. He pointed to the tracing. "This circle is the same size as the spot."

"How do you know?"

"I made a copy of it."

"When?"

"This morning."

"You were at the fair this morning?"

"Yeah. Don't tell anybody, though."

"How'd you get there?"

"I rode my bike." He placed the blue disk and the two circles he'd cut out over his tracing of the spot. "Huh." His first suspicion was wrong. He'd thought maybe it wasn't *possible* to cover the entire spot with the three disks.

"Mom would go nuts if she knew you rode all that way by yourself. It must be ten miles to the fair."

"Eight-point-six. Hmm. They'd have to land perfectly in order to cover the whole thing, but it could be done. Rats." That would've been too easy to detect, he figured. "C'mon, I've got another idea."

They raced back down the stairs and out to the backyard. From the flower bed, Wil plucked a few small stones. Then he put the tracing of the red spot on the picnic table, the stones on top of it, and paced backward nine steps—the distance he estimated between where a player had to stand in front of the Cover the Spot booth and where the table was inside it. Wil tossed the blue disk lightly. It landed fully inside the tracing he'd made of the spot.

"It sails true," he said, collecting the disk. "You try, Sonny. Let me watch."

"How many steps back?

"Nine."

Sonny measured off the distance, eyed the spot, and flicked his wrist. This time the disk landed over the left half of the tracing. "And this one seems exactly like the first two I threw. I don't think there's anything whatever to the theory you're cooking up, Wil."

"I just wanted to make sure I wasn't missing something

obvious," he said, picking up the disk and heading into the garage. Wil's crippled bike was leaning against the wall. Junior had removed the front wheel—the bent rim was on his worktable, a rubber mallet lying next to it, but Wil didn't want to take the time to fix it right now.

"Okay if I use your bike in the morning, Sonny?" Wil asked.

"I wasn't planning on going anywhere at dawn," he said. "You'll be proud of me. Ann-Douglas asked if I wanted to go with her to take pictures of the sunrise, and that was an offer I was able to refuse."

"Hand me that blanket," Wil said, pointing to an old comforter that had been reassigned to miscellaneous outdoor duties. He wrapped the disk in a corner of it and picked up the rubber mallet. He raised his arm and struck the blanket with as much force as he could. The disk didn't crack.

"Want me to try?" Sonny was fit and muscled from having played a year of football and baseball at Cooper County High. He lifted the mallet above his head and brought it down hard.

Wil knew by the sharp sound that the disk had cracked this time. Inside the blanket were three pie-shaped pieces. He peered carefully at each shard. "Dang."

"Were you trying to break that out of frustration?" Sonny asked.

"No, I was looking for a magnet, or some sort of repellent force that would actually prevent it from landing on the spot."

Sonny took a piece of the broken disk and examined it. "Got another idea?"

"No."

"Why is this so important, Wil? Is it just the money? 'Cause I've got money sitting in my sock drawer. I was willing to give it to Junior. I'm willing to give it to you."

"It is the money, but it's not just that." Wil picked up the mallet again and moved to the worktable, where his bike rim was. He started pounding it.

"I know you like a challenge, but you're carrying this pretty far," Sonny said over the hard raps of the mallet against metal. "I mean, I wasn't born the day before I fell off the turnip truck, but I know they didn't invite you to walk into the Cover the Spot booth to trace that thing. You get caught doing something like that, the people who run the fair might call the police. You want to add that to Mom and Dad's dish?"

Wil laid the mallet down. "Plate."

"Dish, plate. Y'know what I mean," Sonny said.

"Doesn't it bother you that these people are cheaters?" Wil asked.

"You don't know that. Maybe it's possible to win, but it's just really hard."

"People can figure out hard if it's fair. There's something else going on."

"Like what?"

"I don't know yet."

"Well, you're running out of time, Detective David. Fair ends Sunday."

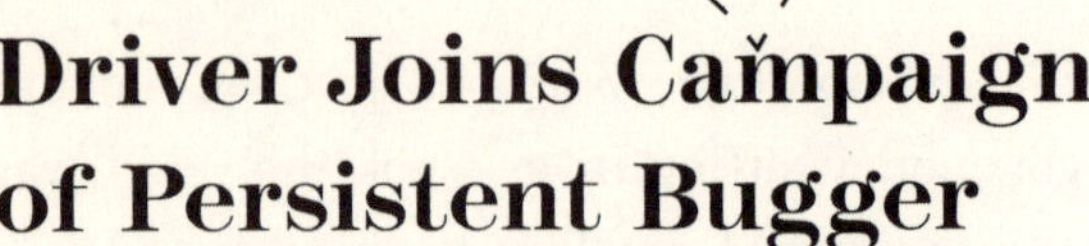

Driver Joins Campaign of Persistent Bugger

Wil was so absorbed in his thoughts about the Cover the Spot game that he didn't hear Manny's truck until it had nearly reached Wayin Road.

"Heard you boys got a petition going," Manny said, climbing down from the cab.

"Where'd you hear that?"

"My daughter told me."

"Was she at the fair last night?"

"Yeah, and that's her last night out for a while. She's supposed to be wearing clothes when she leaves the house."

"Does she have a brown polka-dot bikini?"

"Not anymore." Manny pushed up the rolling gate and pulled a stack of newspapers toward him.

"No offense or anything, Manny, but she must look like her mother."

Manny laughed. "Now that you mention it, she dresses like her mother did, too. Papers are light today." He handed the stack to Wil, who put them on the ground by the bike, then kneeled to slice off the strap holding them together.

"Anyway, tell her I said thanks for signing it."

"You get a lot of people?"

"Almost three hundred names now."

"Dang, Wil. It's true what they say about you." He pulled the gate shut with a *clang*.

Wil stopped what he was doing. "What who says?"

"Folks."

"What do they say?"

"That you are one persistent bugger."

Wil nodded. "You think I'm wasting my time?"

"Maybe. But what else you got to do? Anyway, bring it with you tomorrow—the petition, I mean. I want to sign it, too. And I'll take it with me to the loading dock. Who knows which route they'll cut next, right?" He opened the door to his cab and climbed in.

"Thanks, Manny. I'll do that."

"You keep after 'em, Wil," Manny said, the engine igniting. "They don't call you Wil of Steele for nothing."

Wil got an idea as he was tossing the paper onto Ann-Douglas's porch. It would ruin his time for the morning, but he leaned his bike against a telephone pole and pulled a notepad from the bottom of the canvas sack that held his newspapers. He was giving Ann-Douglas an invitation to interfere in his life. Would he regret it later? Maybe. But he didn't have a choice.

Ann-Douglas,
Can you come to the fair with us today and bring your camera? I need a few pictures of something.
Wil

He stuck the note between the screen door and the doorjamb so somebody would find it when they came out to get the paper.

At home, he wolfed down breakfast before heading to the library. It was a day for notes. Ms. Parsons was off, but she'd left an envelope at the reference desk with his name written on the front.

Wil,

The fax machine is down at the Satellite Valley library, but my friend Annabelle is mailing me a copy of the article you want. I know you wanted it as soon as possible, so I asked her to put it in yesterday's outgoing mail. You can check with me Sunday (we're open 1 to 4) to see if by some miracle it arrived in Saturday afternoon's mail, but it probably won't get here till Monday, I'm afraid. As soon as I get it, I'll put it in an envelope with your name and leave it on my desk so even if I'm not in, you can pick it up.

Ms. Parsons

Ugh, Wil thought. The fair ends Sunday. It might as well not come at all if it didn't arrive till Monday.

A check of his e-mail revealed that Dweeb the Great still hadn't found time to respond. Wil would probably never hear from him. He wrote to Fleur updating her on the petition and the Cover the Spot game. Then he typed in the e-mail address for his Future Physicists of America list. He'd thought about the questions he needed answered as he'd cycled around that morning—about the forces that act on a disk in short flight. What effect weight had on drag. What must be taken into account in terms of aerodynamics. Actually, he was pretty sure he knew the answers to these questions, but he was taking care to apply the principles of the scientific method. He had gathered evidence, measured it, subjected it to testing and reasoning. He had formed hypotheses, found errors, and considered the problem from every angle he could think of, but he could not figure out how the carny could prevent someone with extraordinary accuracy from winning. Yet he was sure there was a way.

Wil pecked out a rough explanation of the game and included the measurements of the disk he'd swiped—he'd estimated its weight at eleven ounces by judging it against various jars and cans in Junior's pantry—and the circumference of the red spot. He hit Send and checked his watch. Wil knew he'd have answers shortly. Physicists, he'd found out, like nothing better than to brainstorm hypotheses, and they spend a lot of time in front of their computers. Even on Saturdays. Physics does not take the weekend off.

He went over to read the newspapers while he waited.

Steele Residents Win Big at Fair

"A twenty-five-dollar gift card from Dweebville Comics!" Trace shouted, waving an envelope as he came out of the exhibition tent where the artwork was on display. His charcoal drawing of a pigeon eating a hot dog on the town green had gotten a white ribbon—third place.

"Junior won, too," Sonny said. "The judge said his Maggie Pies were the best tarts he'd ever tasted, and he looked like a professional sampler."

"My prize came with a little check," Junior said. "Not Pillsbury Bake-Off money, but enough to warm a pocket."

Wil was standing next to Ann-Douglas, who also had a blue ribbon—first place in the juvenile division for her series of time-lapse photographs featuring a boy tossing newspapers from a bike with the sun climbing in the sky behind him. She had gotten a fifty-dollar gift certificate from Vaughn's Camera Shop in Beau Coop.

"I have to remember to tell Maggie that the judges specifically mentioned how much they liked the title in their citation," she said. "They called it 'witty.'"

"What was the title?" Wil asked.

"'The Son(ny) Also Rises!' Get it?"

"Actually, I used to think it was me that got the sun up

every morning," Sonny said. "When I'd start the route, it was dark. By the time I finished, it was light."

"You didn't really think that, did you?" Wil asked.

"Well, then I got the chicken pox, remember? And the sun managed to do its thing without me. But I was sorry to let that idea go, because I liked thinking I was turning on the lights for the day."

"Sonny, that is really moving," Ann-Douglas said. "I think you do turn on the lights for a lot of people."

"Why, thank you, Ann-Douglas," he said.

Wil looked at Trace, hoping somebody would change the subject before he barfed, but it was Junior who came to the rescue.

"Did you check to see if your essay got a ribbon, Wil?" Junior asked.

"What essay?" Ann-Douglas asked. Wil looked puzzled.

"You know—that report you wrote. On the history of Steele," Junior prompted.

"Oh, that," Wil said. The essay could wait. The windfall from the Maggie Pie victory was the opening he needed to advance his plan. "Maybe it's your lucky day, Dad. Why don't you try that Cover the Spot game? You've got as good a chance as anybody."

"What is the essay about?" Ann-Douglas asked.

"Nobody cares. So how about it, Dad? Wanna try that game? The grand prize is a thousand dollars."

Junior's face broke into a bright smile. "I believe I'll do just that, Wil. But let's do the Wild Snake first. I want to grab a bite to eat, but if we're gonna ride that thing, it'd better be on an empty stomach. I'll treat. Who's in?"

"Oh, count me out, Mr. David," Ann-Douglas said. "I rode it twice the other night, and by the end I felt like my brains might have fallen out."

Wil bit his tongue. He needed Ann-Douglas to help him.

"I'll go," Sonny said. "Hey, what happened to Trace?"

Heads swiveled, but Trace had vanished.

"He probably saw something worth doodling," Junior said. "He'll find us. Okay, so how about me and Sonny do the Wild Snake? Meet you by the Cover the Spot game after?"

"That gives us time to look in the 4-H tent for your essay!" Ann-Douglas said.

"Why do you care so much about my essay?" Wil asked.

"Why did you enter if you don't even care who won?"

"I didn't enter it. My mother did."

"Well, if your mother thought it was good enough to enter, you could at least be considerate enough to go and check to see if it won a ribbon."

Dang, this girl was like a thorn in his foot. He made himself stop arguing with her. After all, she was only at the fair because Wil needed a favor, one he knew she was not necessarily going to be willing to do. "Lead on, Ann-Douglas."

The 4-H tent was huge, cooler than the air outside but three times as smelly, and almost as noisy as the screams from people on the Wild Snake, with chickens squawking, geese honking, pigs snuffling, and Ann-Douglas oohing and aahing over every last creature, each of which she felt the need to photograph.

"Oh, my stars. An 'orange Netherland Dwarf,'" she said,

reading the card attached to a rabbit cage. "Doesn't she look like the cuddliest thing you've ever seen?"

"Ann-Douglas, we have to talk," Wil said. "About why I wanted you to bring your camera."

"Oh, oh, oh! I wish I could take him home!" She leaned over a pen that held a pink piglet with a corkscrew tail.

"He stinks. Listen, when we get to the Cover the Spot game, that's when I'm going to need some photos."

"Of the Cover the Spot game? Why?"

He cupped his hand around her ear and gave her instructions.

"What the heck for?" Ann-Douglas asked.

He truly did not want to explain his idea, an idea he had been mulling over all night and day since his last two guesses about how the game was rigged hadn't turned out to be right. Sonny could smooth this over in an instant, but Sonny was on the Wild Snake. So he winked at Ann-Douglas and said "Tell ya why tomorrow?"

She returned his wink with a hard stare. "Why are you being so nice to me?"

"I'm not being nice to you!"

"I don't know why I should do anything for you, Wil David, when it's so plain how much you don't like me."

Sheesh. Girls. What does liking someone have to do with anything? "I like you, Ann-Douglas," he conceded. Sort of. Not really. Wil didn't realize he'd been so obvious. He couldn't help it. She rubbed him the wrong way. With the way she mooned over Sonny, and the way she hogged his mother. And the way his mother mooned over her in return.

"Everyone in your family is nice to me but you."

"Trace isn't nice to you."

"Trace is a senior in high school. He doesn't count."

Wil took a mental deep breath to allow his brain to cool. He could not afford to allow Ann-Douglas to stomp off in a huff, which she appeared to be on the verge of doing. "I promise I will be nicer to you, whatever that means," he said, very calmly, "if you just get the photos I need."

"Sure. I can do that. Easy-peasy. But you're going to owe me."

"Whatever." They had walked beyond the animal area and were now in the section of the tent that had foam-core boards with science projects stapled to them, and tables with embroidered pillows, knitted scarves, and crocheted afghans.

"There's the writing contest." Ann-Douglas pointed to a corkboard with three sets of paper hanging from it, secured by pushpins. She marched right over without waiting for Wil.

"Good gravy, I didn't know you could *write*." She boldly pulled out the pin, handed Wil his blue ribbon, and read the title aloud: "'Wild Hogs and Hairpins: A History of the Founding of Steele, Pennsylvania.'"

Wil was a little shocked he'd won, but he refused to be distracted. He needed to keep his focus on the Cover the Spot game. Meanwhile, Ann-Douglas had plopped down on the spot and was sitting cross-legged on the grassy floor of the tent.

"What are you doing?" Wil asked.

She looked up only to briefly reply, "I'm reading it, of course."

Wild Hogs and Hairpins:
A History of the Founding of Steele, Pennsylvania

by

Wilson Glenn David V

Sixth-grade independent study project

My great-grandfather Wilson Glynn Davidoff founded Steele by accident.

The son of a Scottish mother and a Russian father, Wilson was an inventor. He came to America from England with the pieces of a small machine that could bend wire into different shapes packed inside his steamer trunk. He believed that once the machine was reassembled, he'd be able to manufacture a tiny item with big potential to transform office work. The invention would make him his fortune. Back in those days, people would punch holes and tie ribbons through a stack of papers to hold them together. Sometimes they used straight pins, which occasionally left little spots of blood on otherwise clean pages. While he was an engineering student at the University of Cambridge, my grandfather had a hand in the design of an innovative new product that would change that.

He invented the paper clip. Not just any paper clip but a super-strong one—a double oval made of galvanized steel.

According to the diaries of his wife (and my great-grandmother), Mary David, he had sent diagrams and samples of his unique design to several

American manufacturers. The owners of Steel Office Products in Pittsburgh, Pennsylvania, responded immediately. This is a copy of the original telegram, borrowed from my great-grandmother's scrapbooks (Volume 1):

WILSON G DAVIDOFF
C/O SMITH & SMITH MFG

IMMEDIATE NEED FOR YOUR MACHINE STOP FUNDS FOR PASSAGE TO PITTS PA ARRIVING BY WIRE TRANSFER STOP REPLY WITH ARRIVAL DATE

B J MELLON
STEEL OFFICE PRODUCTS

My great-grandfather booked passage on the next boat leaving Southampton. On the ship he met Mary, who (this is important) had just gotten her curly red hair cut into a new style. They were married by a chaplain as the boat chugged into New York Harbor, where an immigration clerk trimmed the *off* from my great-grandfather's Russian last name and pronounced the newlyweds, "Wilson and Mary David." They honeymooned on the Pennsylvania Railroad between New York and Pittsburgh.

My great-grandfather settled his new bride at a boardinghouse on Monongahela Avenue and strode across the cobblestoned streets of Pittsburgh to meet his new employers. Later, my great-grandmother recorded her husband's version of events in her diary:

The company president, B. J. Mellon, told Wilson to have a seat. "I've got bad news, Davidoff," he said.

Wilson needed to tell him about the name change immediately, of course. "Actually, it's just David now, sir," he said, but this Mellon fellow was, perhaps, not too bright, because the next thing he said was, "Take a look at this, Dave."

He pushed a copy of an article clipped from the Pittsburgh Post-Gazette a week earlier across the desk. I've included it here:

Connecticut Inventor Wins U.S. Patent for Revolutionary "Paper Clip"

By Peyton Baldwin
Associated Press

WASHINGTON, DC (Nov. 9) -- A Connecticut man has been awarded U.S. Patent No. 636,272 for a device that holds several sheets of paper together by means of pressure.

William D. Middlebrook, of Waterbury, calls his invention the "paper clip." "It leaves the paper intact and can be easily removed," Middlebrook said. "No more straight pins or strings. The paper clip is a wonder of simplicity and function—just what we need at the dawn of the twentieth century."

Middlebrook has also invented a machine to produce the paper clip and is in negotiations to sell his machine to Cushman & Denison, a leading manufacturer of office staples.

My great-grandfather wondered if Middlebrook's design was really as good as his own. Did he use *galvanized* steel? Had he blunted the metal edges to prevent damage to the paper? According to my great-grandmother's account, Mellon apparently didn't care to find out whether or not my great-grandfather's design was superior.

Mellon told my dear Wilson, "You're a day late and a dollar short, Dave." (That he called him "Dave" a second time seemed to upset Wilson almost as much as the fact that the Connecticut fellow had gotten to the patent office first!) Mellon said they wouldn't make Wilson reimburse the company for bringing him to America, but there was no job for him there anymore, either. We were both stunned!

My great-grandfather staggered out of Steel Office Products, the newspaper clipping in his hand.

Mary bought that day's issue of the *Pittsburgh Post-Gazette* with the few coins they had between them, and scoured the Help Wanted ads. She found one (which she also saved; Scrapbooks, Volume 1) and read it aloud.

FARM MANAGER
IMMEDIATE NEED

Manager needed to run 60-acre farm, sw of Dweebville. Married couple preferred. Inquiries to Louis M. Jepeway, Esq. Barrister Bldg., Allegheny St.

My great-grandfather was concerned. "Does it say if it's a farm with animals or a farm with vegetables?" He didn't have much experience with animals, except for the time a stray dog had chased him to school in St. Andrew's parish, trying to steal the lunch he was carrying in a sack. But the ad didn't specify, so they spiffed themselves up and asked the woman who owned the boardinghouse for directions.

Jepeway, the attorney, was thrilled to see them. The widowed owner of the farm, Bertram Tucker, had been running the place alone and taken ill. While he was hospitalized no one had been feeding his hogs.

"Hogs?" my great-grandfather asked.

"So you can see the urgency," Jepeway said. "I'll advance you twenty-five dollars so you can hire a car to take you there," he added, skipping over the part where he said they had gotten the job.

"Thank you, sir," Wilson said. "But we're economizing. The bus would be fine."

"There's no bus service to Tucker's Farm, Mr. David," Jepeway said.

"Oh," Mary said, the realization of why a married couple was preferred dawning on her. There probably wasn't *any* kind of service at Tucker's Farm. At least a married couple meant you weren't there alone with the hogs.

"When would you need us to start?" my great-grandfather asked.

"Yesterday," Jepeway said. "How soon can you be there?"

"Today?" Wilson answered, looking at Mary for reassurance. She nodded.

"Capital," the attorney said. "Don't know what you'll find when you arrive. Tucker's health was deteriorating before this latest knockout punch. Good luck." He pressed the key to the farmhouse into my great-grandfather's hand. "I believe you'll need it." My great-grandmother remembers he practically pushed them out of his office. When the door clicked shut behind them, Wilson had a pinched expression on his face that suggested he was already imagining the smell.

It didn't take long for my great-grandparents to nearly run the farm into the ground but, to be fair, they were given a head start. There were hogs, dozens and dozens of them—or there had been. When no one fed them, the hogs had apparently staged a riot, battered down their pen, and went rooting for food in the woodlots that surrounded the farm.

My great-grandparents spent their first week repairing fences and the following week hog calling in the woods to retrieve the herd. Some of the animals had gone native and became aggressive when Wilson approached. One charged at his neatly creased pants, so Wilson darted up a tree, something he hadn't done since his school days at St. Andrew's.

There was also a kitchen garden that needed weeding, hay that needed threshing, a field of wheat that needed harvesting, two dehydrated horses, confused chickens sitting on mounds of uncollected eggs, and a homely hound who had apparently kept himself alive by rolling eggs off the bottom shelf of the chicken coop with his nose and then lapping up the broken pieces, shell and all. The smell of the place was far worse than my great-grandfather had imagined at the lawyer's office in Pittsburgh.

"I don't know if we can do this," he once confessed to my great-grandmother. He had been a natural at engineering, analytical and meticulous; a man who took care to keep his fingernails clean.

"But what choice do we have?" she answered. This wasn't the future she'd imagined for herself, either, when she'd agreed to marry a soon-to-be-rich inventor.

So they kept at it, up with the sun every day, working on a list of chores two people could never accomplish by themselves. Still, after slopping the hogs, my great-grandfather always tried to spend an hour in the workshop he'd set up in one corner of the barn. His dream of a fortune in metal clips scattered like so many sheets of unclamped paper in the wind, he was determined to think up something else. But the first device he made was something simply to make Mary happier. He rejiggered his wire-forming machine to make her new hairpins. She'd had her hair cut short in London before leaving—a new style that required twisting each wet strand into a tight curlicue and securing it with a pin before she went to bed. The pins she'd brought with her had lost their tension, and there was nowhere to buy new ones. Consequently, her curls often had a sproingy appearance that added to her despair, for Mary had not envisioned a life spent hoeing rows of peas, nor feeding chickens, nor days on end with bad hair.

That might have been her fate had she not, several months after the Davids' arrival, driven the cart into the farmer's market in Dweebville one Saturday morning with corn and eggs to sell. Her red hair, full of curly life from having slept with it coiled around the pins Wilson had made, framed her face. Her cheeks had roses from the open-air ride. She had a secret, too—a baby on the way, the child who would become Wilson Glenn David the First, later known simply as "Doc," because of his knack for taking broken things apart and figuring out how to fix them.

"Mornin', Mrs. David," the tomato seller called out. "You didn't have to dress up just for us."

Dress up? Mary thought.

Then, as she was setting out her baskets: "Why, Mrs. David, you look like the bloom of youth." This from the hired man who hauled in strawberries from a farm near Coop de Ville.

"Thank you, Wes," she said. Is it the baby, she thought?

Finally, while packing an order of two dozen eggs and ten ears of corn, a customer she didn't know at all leaned over Mary's produce to draw her attention and whispered, "May I ask you a personal question?"

Goodness. She wasn't ready to share her news with strangers. She wasn't even showing yet.

"Where do you get your hair done?" the woman wanted to know.

"Oh, my hair," Mary said in relief, touching her fingers to either side of her head as if to make sure it was still there. "Why, I do it myself."

"You can't!" the woman exclaimed.

"I do!" Mary assured her.

"But how do you get it to keep its curl so well?"

Mary reached into the pocket of her apron and produced two sturdy metal pins. "My husband made these for me—see the crinkle on the top side? I wash it at night, twist a strand, and secure it with one of these. The crinkle puts a nice wave into it. I just pick it out with my fingers in the morning."

"Miraculous! But—you say he *made* those pins?"

"Why, yes, he's an engineer. He invented the paper cl—"

The woman cut her off. "Can he make some for *me*?"

Before the year was out, the proceeds from the Davids' hairpin business exceeded the money they made from farming. The ladies at the farmer's market had cousins in Pittsburgh and sisters in Philadelphia. Miss Altoona became Miss Pennsylvania at the state pageant in Harrisburg with a hairdo made possible by Steele Hairpins—that was the name Wilson gave them, adding an extra *e* to the name of the company that had brought him to America because he thought it contributed panache. At the time, he had a vague hope that the office-products company might find out about the hairpins and change their minds about employing him, but there was no need. Mr. Tucker passed away without ever saying good-bye to his hound or his hogs, and Wilson and Mary bought his property from the estate. They sold the hogs—*Good riddance!* Wilson thought as the brutes rode off in a cart—turned the barn into a factory, and hired a crew out of Dweebville to build Wayin Road. They renamed Tucker's Farm for the product it was now producing: Steele Hairpins. Demand increased exponentially over the next decade; the Davids hired a staff, then a workforce. The trip into and out of the valley could be treacherous during the winter months, so Wilson had homes built for his workers, and a small downtown where they could shop for life's essentials. He developed a town square with a clock tower and a gazebo at one end and a baseball field at the other, where the Steele Knights took on company teams from other mills and factories. When *The Cooper County Caller* came to Steele seeking someone to distribute the newspaper in the new community, my great-grandfather felt like he had accomplished something big. He had created a family, a product, a factory, and a town big enough to warrant the attention of the newspaper. He volunteered to deliver the papers himself.

When the Great Depression hit, belts were tightened, but no one at Steele Hairpins was laid off. The Davids forgot how much they didn't like farmwork and set aside acreage for a community garden. "Make ourselves a little more self-sufficient," Wilson suggested.

Mary's baby grew up and took over the job of delivering newspapers from his father, until his son, named Junior, grew old enough to take over. Then Junior had three sons, each of whom got the route when he turned twelve. My turn to have the route is just one year away, and I will proudly take on the tradition of bringing the news to the town that my great-grandfather founded: Steele, Pennsylvania.

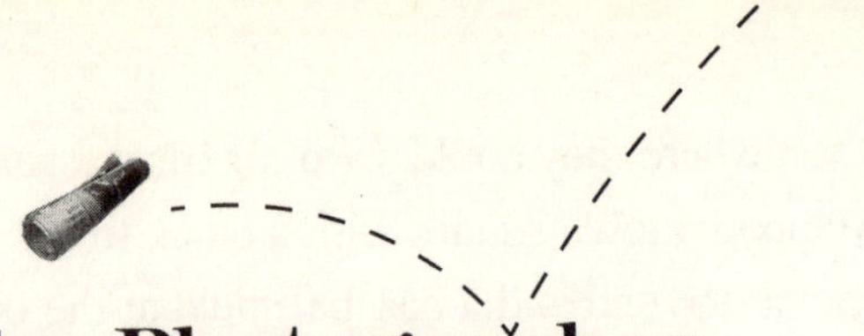

Pesky Photographer Makes Key Observation

The crowd in front of the game seemed bigger than ever when Wil and Ann-Douglas arrived, looking for Junior and Sonny.

"I thought your thing was science," Ann-Douglas said.

"Thank you for the compliment?" Wil responded.

"I mean, I knew you were good at science and math, but . . ."

"A lot of that stuff came straight out of my great-grandmother's diaries. That's why there's a full page of endnotes."

"Oh, well, you shouldn't pass it off as your own if you didn't write it yourself."

"I included where I got the information from, Ann-Douglas."

"But you made it sound like a story. Like a story *you* wrote," Ann-Douglas insisted.

Why? What had he done to have to deal with this exasperating person? "I did write it. I read what she wrote and all the newspaper articles and then I made a report out of it. There's Sonny."

"I think your great-grandmother should get the blue ribbon and the gift card," Ann-Douglas continued.

"Well, what about you? You think you're the first person to ever take a photo of the sunrise?"

"What does that have to do with anything?"

"I've seen plenty of photos of sunrises before you started taking them. I guess you're trying to pass that off as your idea."

"I get up to take photos of the sunrise every day because the light conditions are different each day. That's what they taught us at art camp about how to learn to truly observe something."

"Do you give your camp credit on every photo?"

"Oh, Wil David!" She stamped her foot. "It's not the same thing and you know it."

"What's got you two all fired up?" Junior asked.

"I won the blue ribbon for my essay." Wil showed his father his ribbon.

"Wow! Your mother will flip," Junior said. "She's been hoping to have a writer in the family."

"Rewriter," Ann-Douglas grumbled.

"Sonny coming?" Wil asked.

Junior nodded in the direction of the ride area, where Sonny had been corralled by a circle of girls from Cooper County High.

"You want to try to pry him away from his fan club?" Junior nodded in Sonny's direction.

"Sure. Are you going to get in line to play the game?" Wil asked.

"Indeed I am," Junior said, rubbing his hands together like he had dice in his palms and already knew he'd roll snake eyes. "I'm feeling lucky."

"We'll wait over on the side where we can see you when it's your turn," Wil said. Ann-Douglas was looking highly uncooperative, so he took her by the elbow and guided her in the direction he wanted her to go.

"Cut it out, Wil," she said, jerking her elbow out of his reach.

"Ann-Douglas, it's important to be as unobtrusive as possible."

"Speak English, please. Not all of us are homeschooled by Mrs. Noah Webster."

"Don't let the carny see you taking the photos."

"And you just want pictures of his hands?"

"Right." Wil had decided that whatever the guy was doing had to involve that mysterious box with the red button. What else could it be? He'd watched him several dozen times now. He'd measured the spot, the disks, cracked one open, looked under the table—the only thing left was that box. And Wil had seen him move toward it and away from it every time somebody did well on the first two throws.

"Is this some kind of criminal activity, Wil? My parents will not take kindly to me getting mixed up in any shenanigans, no matter how smart you are."

"No shenanigans. Don't do anything to attract his attention. Just carefully watch his hands." As he whispered these instructions to Ann-Douglas he had a sudden jolt: Madame Prévu—her warning! What was it? *Careful watching.* Wil felt a shiver run down his spine. Could this be what she had meant?

"I just realized what I want in exchange for doing this,"

Ann-Douglas whispered forcefully, snapping Wil out of his momentary trance.

"What?"

"I want you to get Sonny to take me to the Harvest Dance in October. He'll do it if you tell him to."

"Ann-Douglas, Sonny is going to be a high school sophomore. Even I couldn't convince him to go to a dance at Coop de Ville Middle."

"Then *you'll* have to take me."

"Oh, no. I take dances off for the school year." Out of the corner of his eye, he could see Junior giving his five dollars to the carny. He would need Ann-Douglas to get into position to take the pictures right now.

"There isn't anything else I want."

"Okay, okay." Maybe he would be sick that day. "I'll take you, but I don't know how to dance."

"We can sign you up for cotillion in September."

"Dancing lessons? Have you lost your mind???" he asked, way too loud. He quickly checked to make sure he hadn't attracted the carny's notice. He hadn't. The earsplitting shrieks from the rides area had drowned him out.

"Pinkie swear." Ann-Douglas fisted her hand with just the little finger sticking out.

"Just for the dance. No cotillion."

"Okay, just the dance. But you have to buy me a corsage."

Ah, jeez. Was a thousand dollars worth this? "Okay. Dance. Flowers. That's it." He hooked his pinkie with Ann-Douglas's.

She smiled and brought the camera to her eye, pressing

a button that moved the lens in and out. "I have to admit I do like this Harriet the Spy stuff."

"Just get the photos, Ann-Douglas."

When it was Junior's turn, Wil gestured for Ann-Douglas to move closer. His first toss landed entirely over the spot, covering a good third of the center and right side.

"Woo-hoo, boy," the carny said. "Good starts don't come any better than that, folks!"

Wil watched the carny's hands. He had two blue disks in his left palm. His right hand was in the pocket of his pants—white carpenter's pants that, Wil noted, he'd been wearing for three nights straight.

The carny handed Junior his second disk. This toss was perfect, too. It landed just north and west of the first one, covering the entire top of the spot and the center-left side. Wil glanced in the mirror. All that showed of the spot now was a red wedge at the bottom.

Hoots and cheers came from the bystanders. Somebody in the back called out, "Don't forget about that twenty you owe me, Junior!" Laughter rippled through the crowd.

Ann-Douglas nudged Wil's arm. "Is he gonna win?"

Wil saw the carny glance at the table, then move closer to the counter. He had the last disk in his hands. Just like the night before with Sonny, the carny seemed to be in no rush to give Junior his third disk.

From the side of the booth, Wil had a view almost no one else had, and he saw what the carny did next—pick up his right leg slightly and lean into the counter. Wil knew exactly what he was doing. He was using his knee to push the red button on the metal box hidden under the counter.

"Did you see that?" Ann-Douglas asked. She said this without taking her eye from the viewfinder on her camera. The camera whirred as she snapped picture after picture in rapid succession.

The carny was asking for quiet.

"Wil," she whispered urgently.

"I saw it, Ann-Douglas," he hissed back at her. "Take photos."

"But do you still want me to take them of just his hands?" she asked. Wil, intent in his focus, ignored her.

The carny handed the third disk to Junior. Over the heads of the crowd, Wil saw a large man come into view. He stood out because he was wearing a white suit and a ten-gallon hat. Next to him was the security guard and Jake, the garbage-eating dog.

Do they sic the dog on winners? Wil wondered.

"I'm gonna take a picture of his feet, too, Wil."

Ann-Douglas's comments finally registered with him. "What?" But it was too late to do anything but watch. Junior let the disk go. It hovered in the air and landed softly. If it had fallen any harder, Wil might have missed what happened. If Ann-Douglas, *pesky Ann-Douglas,* hadn't planted the idea in his subconscious, he might not have thought to look down as the disk landed, perfectly, over the bottom third of the spot.

But he did look down. Down at the carny's legs. Not his hands. Not the alarm button. He looked at the man's legs—at just the moment Junior's third disk hit its mark. How could he have missed it before? He had overthought it, giving these jerks credit for more intelligence than they had.

He knew immediately what would happen next.

"Aw, that's a shame!" The carny banged his palm on the counter.

Everyone watching seemed to lurch forward at once, craning their necks for a better look, and there it was: the teensiest triangle of red on the left side of the spot. The crowd cried out collectively, but Wil could hear Junior's deep groan over the rest.

"So close!" the carny said, sticking out his hand to shake Junior's. "You ought to try again."

Oh, no he shouldn't, Wil thought. *I'M* next. And I'm going home tomorrow night with a thousand dollars in my pocket.

Photographs Reveal Nothing But the Truth

"I had that money spent already," Junior said. People swirled around him, encouraging him to give the game another try.

"You were closer than anybody else I've seen play, Junior," a man in a plaid shirt said.

"Easy come, easy go, right, kids?" He turned, smiling, to address Wil and Ann-Douglas.

Wil was fuming. Rotten crooks!

Sonny had somehow pried himself loose from his harem. "You figure it out, Wil?" he whispered.

Wil nodded. "Ann-Douglas, did you get a picture?"

She was scrolling backward through the images she'd captured. The three of them moved away from Junior and the throng around him.

"I got a picture, but you can't see anything." Wil and Sonny crowded in on either side of her, but she was right—you could see the carny's leg, but that was it.

"You took pictures of his leg?" Sonny asked. "What's that gonna prove?"

Junior had extracted himself from the crowd. "Whatcha got there, Ann-Douglas?"

Ann-Douglas let the camera hang around her neck and pretended to have a scratch that needed itching. "Just pictures from the fair, Mr. David."

"We might need a video camera," Wil muttered, not loud enough for anybody but himself to hear. "And we definitely need the police."

"We better round up Trace. How 'bout I treat for frozen custard while we look for him?" Junior offered.

"Sounds like a plan to me," Sonny said, and as soon as Sonny agreed, Ann-Douglas did, too.

"I'll just wait for you at the car," Wil said.

"You sure?" Junior asked, but Wil was already heading toward the exit. He was making a list in his head—a long list—of all the things he needed to do before tomorrow night, the last night of the fair.

New Carrier Calls Emergency Meeting

Wil had the petition for Manny when the truck arrived Sunday morning.

"Morning, Manny. I'm going to ask all of my subscribers to come to the Town Council meeting tomorrow to talk about what else we can do to get *The Caller* to reverse their decision. Here's some flyers you can pass out, just in case any of the other carriers are interested in coming."

"My, my. I see you had your Wheaties already," Manny said, smiling. He took the petition and the flyers and laid them on the front seat of his truck. "When I get the other guys to sign, I'll spread the word. You by yourself?"

"Sonny's working on his beauty sleep." Sonny and Trace had stayed up late watching a movie after they got home from the fair. Wil went straight upstairs and made the flyers, urging everyone concerned about *The Caller*'s decision to attend Monday's Town Council meeting. Walking back to the car the night before, he imagined, for the first time, winning that one thousand dollar prize. But his next thought surprised him. He wasn't dreaming about the laptop he would buy. He was thinking about how getting a computer wouldn't make him feel better about losing the newspaper route. He wanted the route more than he wanted the laptop, he realized. But why? He had his blue ribbon in his front pocket and his rolled-up essay in his back pocket. He had always felt proud that he lived in a town his great-grandfather had founded. But that town was suffering now. When the hairpin factory closed, other businesses had gone belly-up with it, because people who lost their jobs didn't have money to shop, or had left town to find jobs elsewhere, like the family of Ann-Douglas's friend, Olivia. Losing the route felt like another sucker punch. Wil just couldn't let another bad thing happen to Steele. He wrote out copies of the flyer until his hand cramped so badly he worried he'd have trouble flinging the Sunday papers.

Manny set the last stack down on the pavement by Wil's bike. "Don't know how Spike can claim we're losing money when these papers are heavier than ever. There's two inches of circulars."

"Can you bring the petition back with you tomorrow morning?" Wil asked. "I want to have it at the meeting."

"Sure thing, Wil."

"Thanks, Manny. Thanks for everything."

"No thanks necessary. Next I'm gonna suggest you work on world hunger, though, Wil. We'd have it licked by a week from Friday."

Wil laughed and waved goodbye. Then he sat down cross-legged on the pavement and began tucking his handwritten notices about the Town Council meeting inside every Sunday edition. He had one other note, too, this one for Judge Salzberg, telling her he'd be by later to discuss a matter of extreme urgency, and requesting that she plan to meet him at the fair that night at six-forty-five, in front of the Cover the Spot booth. He would put it on top of her newspaper and hand-deliver it inside her screen door so she would be certain to see it.

But as he pedaled up Judge Salzberg's street, he could already see Ann-Douglas waiting on her porch. She stood when she saw him coming and ran down the walk. Wil braked and swung his leg over his seat, carefully balancing the bike against a tree in the swale so it would lean but not tip, or spill all his precisely arranged papers.

"Wil, I wanted to talk to you," Ann-Douglas said.

"Will you see Judge Salzberg today?"

"Probably. I see her almost every day."

"Can you give her a note from me? I was just going to leave it with her newspaper, but I don't want her to miss it. It's super-important," he said.

"Sure," she said, taking the note from Wil's outstretched hand.

"Here's your newspaper, too," he added.

"Thanks. Listen," she started.

Wil thought she looked sad, but maybe she was just tired. It was way too early for anybody who didn't have a newspaper route to be up. "I better get going with the papers. . . ."

"Wait," she said quickly. "I need to apologize."

"About the photos? Not at all. I should thank you for pointing out that I was looking at the wrong thing. You did learn a lot about observing at art camp."

"No, no, not about the photos. About your essay. About accusing you of cheating because you used your great-grandmother's diary."

"I've forgotten about it already, Ann."

"I thought about it all night, and what I kept coming back to was the summer reading contest. Do you remember?"

Wil remembered it clearly. "You mean the one right after you moved here and your parents painted the house purple?"

"Right. It's not purple, Wil, it's periwinkle."

"Oh. Periwinkle. Would Mrs. Noah Webster say that was another word for purple?"

"Yes. I'm sorry about that comment, too. But my point is, that was the last time you were in the summer reading contest."

Wil didn't respond.

"Was it because I won?"

"Of course not," he said, too quickly. Was it? he wondered.

"But Ms. Parsons told me that before I got here, you won every year."

"I just got interested in other things," he said, but Wil remembered he had not liked losing. There had always been competition with his brothers, but even though they were older, he won a lot. Then came this new girl, out of the blue, who won the reading contest by a landslide. Wil winced at the memory. He remembered now getting home after the winners had been announced and going straight to his room so no one would see that he was upset.

"The thing is, Wil, that first year, I had help winning."

"What do you mean?"

"That summer I was going into third grade, so it was

four years ago." From inside the house, a sharp *ding* sounded. "The cinnamon rolls! Can you wait a minute? You're here earlier than Sonny usually was." She did not wait for an answer but scampered back up the walk and inside the house before Wil could even say, "Sure." He rearranged the papers in his sack for better balance to get his mind off that summer, four years ago, when his mother had given out the awards for the summer reading contest and befriended Ann-Douglas. He hadn't just finished second to the new kid. It turned out his mom had always wanted a daughter. "I saved all of my Betsy-Tacy books, hoping one day there'd be someone to share them with, and now there is," Wil had heard his mother say. He wondered what was so special about the Betsy-Tacy books and even tried reading one. He didn't get very far. It was about girls, and ladies who left calling cards.

Ann-Douglas backed out of the screen door, carrying a tray. "I brought you a glass of milk, too."

Wil was hungry, and the cinnamon scent carried on the breeze to the sidewalk. He went forward to the porch, where Ann-Douglas had put the tray down on a table. "They smell good," he said, picking a roll from the plate. "There's no textured vegetable stuff in this, is there?"

She shook her head. "Anyway, the thing about the summer reading contest, Wil, that first summer?"

Ann-Douglas looked away from Wil. She seemed to be trying to screw up her nerve to make some major confession. Wil felt awkward yet curious. Did she cheat?

"The thing is," she said, sucking in a big breath, "I couldn't really read yet."

Hmm, Wil thought. "How could you win the summer reading contest if you couldn't read?"

"I had gotten through second grade by memorizing whole stories. I would just read the same ones over and over again. I never chose any book that didn't have pictures, because the pictures would help me fake it."

"So all those books you wrote on your log you didn't really read?"

She shook her head. Wil felt terrible, because now there was a tear leaking out of her eye. Here was another good reason not to chitchat with customers before sunup.

"I tried to read some of them by myself, but my mother or father, or even Judge Salzberg, mostly read them *to* me."

"But, wait, you're the world's biggest reader, second only to my mother," he said.

"Well, I can read now. I mean, I think that contest is what did it. Somebody read to me every night, and by the end of the summer, I could read a whole chapter of a book with no pictures at all by myself. And then I wanted to be able to read them like Judge Salzberg does, putting on voices and making them scary or silly."

"That's not cheating, Ann-Douglas."

"And I don't think what you did was cheating either. I was just jealous. I would like to be able to write like that."

Both of them got very quiet. In the sky, two birds flew side by side, the push of their wings against the heavy air the only sound. Ann-Douglas had been brave to tell him about the summer reading contest, he realized.

"I'm sorry if I haven't really ever been much of a friend, Ann-Douglas," he said.

"Same with me," she said.

"Mind if I have another cinnamon roll? They're super good."

"Omigosh, no!" she said. "I made them for you."

Librarian's Comment Sparks Action

At twelve-thirty, Wil was outside the library waiting for Ms. Parsons's car to pull up. The library opened at one on Sunday.

"This must be incredibly important, Wil," she said, letting him follow her into the building, switching on the lights, putting her handbag under the counter, and retreating to an office behind it. Wil could see her pull a stack of envelopes and magazines from a cubbyhole along one wall. She flipped through them quickly, then put them back in the mail slot.

She shook her head as she came out of the office. "It would've been a miracle to arrive in one day," she said.

Wil knew that. Still, he was disappointed.

"I've been thinking about *The Caller*, Wil. It really troubles me. I mean, if any town in the world needs newspaper delivery, it's Steele. Our residents don't have cable, and a lot of them can't afford a satellite dish. Most of them don't even have computers. There are four channels on the TV when the reception is good, but I mean, really, I think most of them still rely on the paper for vital information."

Wil felt guilty listening to this. Not that he didn't agree. But he had to admit, it had taken him a while to see that the newspaper's decision was bigger than him, bigger than the loss of one boy's job. It was about his whole town losing something. Something important.

"Anyway, I got your note about the meeting. I'll be there. I'm so happy to see you fight for this—it's just terrible to be written off as if we're too small to matter," Ms. Parsons said. "If it wasn't the newspaper that was involved, somebody would call the newspaper to complain about it."

Wil was about to tell Ms. Parsons about the sit-in he was planning if the petition didn't work when he was brought up short by the last thing she'd said. "Call the newspaper?"

"Why, yes. If the telephone company or the electric utility unilaterally decided one day it wasn't profitable to provide service to Steele, wouldn't we call the newspaper, try to whip up some fury over that?"

"Oh, Ms. Parsons!" And this time Wil couldn't help himself. He hugged her. "That's a great idea! May I borrow your phone?"

"Why, of course," she said, looking puzzled but pleased.

Wil ran to get the newspaper. He knew where to find the phone number he needed inside it. Ms. Parsons had gone to the kitchenette to start a pot of coffee when Wil's call went through—to *The Satellite Valley News.*

"Newsroom, Joey Rento."

"May I speak to Phoebe Flowers?"

"I'm afraid *she* doesn't have to work on Sundays."

"Can you get her a message?"

"You want to leave it on her voice mail? The Pirates are playing the Yankees. Interleague game. It's about to start."

"Will she check her voice mail today?"

"There's no guarantee, since she, unlike other, more deserving people with actual things to do like go to Pittsburgh for a ball game, is *off* on Sunday. What's this about?"

"It's a follow-up to a story she wrote a few weeks ago, about the Cover the Spot game at the Livingston County Fair."

"Keep talking," Rento said.

"Well, could you please call her and tell her if she wants another front page exclusive to be at the Cooper County Fairgrounds tonight at six-forty-five."

"Okay, but where at the fair?"

"In front of the Cover the Spot game," Wil said. "And tell her to bring a photographer."

Wil went home then and found Junior in the garage, pounding on Wil's bicycle rim with the rubber mallet. He watched him for a moment, then took a deep breath and made some noise so he wouldn't startle him.

"Oh, hey, Wil," Junior said, turning. "What's up?"

"Dad," he said. "I have something to tell you." And it poured out—what Wil knew, how he knew it, what he had planned.

He needed another ride to the fair, after all.

Local Boy Vies for Grand Prize at Fair's Cover the Spot Game

Wil focused on the thin red crescent still visible on the table inside the booth. His first two disks had covered all but one curved slice of the spot. All he had to do was land the third disk over this last piece, covering the spot completely, and the money was his—a thousand dollars in cash.

"This is for the big prize, folks!" the carny yelled. "All the marbles."

"Give him some room, please," Sonny said. The crowd inched back before crowding in again.

"Wil, don't overthink this," Junior whispered.

Sonny leaned in close. "Show 'em what a kid from Steele can do, Wil."

Wil gave his brother a solemn nod. He transferred the third blue disk from his right hand to his left and dried his palm on his shorts. Then he shut out all the other noise around him like he was turning off lights on his way to bed. The music from the merry-go-round. The screams from the Wild Snake. People talking behind him, speculating on his odds.

Leaning forward slightly, Wil narrowed his eyes at the red slash he had to hit. He wished Madame Prévu was nearby with her horseshoe. Instead he crossed two fingers of his left hand, for luck. Then he gripped the disk firmly and flicked his wrist evenly.

The blue disk sailed in slow motion, spinning through the short space between Wil and the table. The crowd held its breath and so did Wil—until the disk landed smoothly, squarely on top of the small patch of red.

"Yeehaw!" came the first cheer, from over to Wil's right, and then the whooping and hollering got so loud it *did* drown out the screams from the Wild Snake. Junior thumped Wil's back. Sonny caught him around the waist and lifted him off the ground. Wil was about to put his arms in the air in a triumphant V when the carny rapped the counter sharply with his knuckles.

"Aw, that's a shame." The carny was shaking his head.

"But he got it!" someone in the crowd called.

"Naw, he didn't." The carny acted like he was real disappointed. "Look." He pointed to the mirror above the table.

"Well, I'll be danged. . . ." Junior said. Wil *had* covered the red slice he was aiming for, but did he knock one of the other disks out of position in the process? There was now a toenail clipping of red visible at the other side of the spot—a part that had been covered completely before Wil's third and final toss.

"Sorry, kid," the carny said, extending his hand. "But this ain't horseshoes or hand grenades. Close ain't good enough."

Local Judge Rules for Truth, Justice

"Wait just a minute!" came a shout.

The throng parted for Judge Salzberg, who had a Cooper County sheriff's deputy on either side of her.

The carny's face paled, and he seemed to be searching over the heads of the crowd for either someone to save him, or an exit.

"You say this boy did not win?" Judge Salzberg asked.

"Ma'am, you can see for yourself—look in the mirror! See that strip of red? He's got to cover the whole spot to win the thousand dollars. It's not my rule, it's Mr. Bates's, and here he is now!" The carny pointed to a man in a white suit and a ten-gallon hat who was striding purposefully down the midway. People stepped aside to let him pass.

"Hello, folks!" said Bates, all cheerful, clapping people's backs as he worked his way to the front. "What seems to be the trouble here? We can't have trouble at the fair, not at *my* fair, no sir."

"I am Circuit Court Judge Ruth Salzberg, and these gentlemen from the Cooper County Sheriff's Department are here at my request. Are you the owner, sir?" Judge Salzberg asked him.

"I am, indeed, F. James Bates, president of Bates Family

Fun Carnival, the number-one provider of touring, wholesome entertainment for nearly ninety years," he said in a bluster. "How can I help?"

"This young man," Judge Salzberg said, taking Wil by the shoulders, "appeared to everyone in this crowd, including me, to have covered the spot entirely. But somehow the arrangement of the blue disks looks slightly different now."

"Well, the mirror doesn't lie, Your Honor. You can clearly see—"

"Then you won't mind if we ask your employee Carl here—or is it '*Curly*'?—to come out front and take a look himself, will you?"

Wil's heart was beating so fast he had to remember to keep breathing. He barely noticed at all when a tall woman sidled right up behind him. He didn't see the man she came with—a guy with a camera around his neck—at all. The photographer had set up in Wil's favorite spot, over to the right of the booth.

"That's not going to change the results, Your Honor. We can all clearly see—"

"Humor me," Judge Salzberg said firmly, though she didn't look like she thought any of this was funny.

"Sir, please have your employee step out of the booth, right now," said the deputy on Judge Salzberg's left.

Jimbo Bates grimaced. "Curl—I mean, Carl, do as the officer says."

"Boss, you know I can't—"

"Do it."

Quiet covered the fair like a blanket. The crowd around

the Cover the Spot game had gotten bigger, spilling out on every side, but no one uttered a sound. The ride operators had sensed something big was going on and paused the merry-go-round and the Tilt-A-Whirl. The Wild Snake had stopped its serpentine path through the sky. It was like the entire fair was holding its breath.

"It's your funeral," the carny said. In a flash, he undid his carpenter's pants and stepped out of them.

The crowd gasped as one. Mothers clamped their hands over their children's eyes. An eruption of hoots and catcalls filled the air as the carny hopped over the counter, leaving his pants behind.

Judge Salzberg retained complete composure. "Miss Flowers," she said, looking over Wil's head at the tall woman standing behind him. "Is your photographer in place?"

"He sure is, Your Honor." She pointed to the man with the camera, who was clicking away furiously.

"Deputy Davidson, will you kindly retrieve *Carl*'s pants? Surely he doesn't want to go to jail in his boxer shorts."

"Yes, Your Honor." The other deputy had the carny by the arm.

Deputy Davidson noisily clambered into the booth. He picked up the pants and as he did the Cover the Spot table *moved with them.* Murmuring started among the people closest to the booth.

The deputy took the pants' right leg in his hand, and now the people at the front of the crowd could easily see a length of clear nylon thread running from the pants to one leg of the table.

Deputy Davidson then turned the pant leg inside out

and showed the inside hem to Judge Salzberg, Jimbo Bates, Wil of Steele, and his whole family. All of them could clearly see that the fishing line ran from the table leg to the pants, where it was affixed to the inside hem by a rusty, slightly bent, extra-large, double-oval paper clip.

‹ satellite valley news exclusive ›

Corruption Exposed at Carnival Fair Game

Fair Owner and Carnival Worker Taken into Custody

By Phoebe Flowers, Staff Writer

(Dweebville, July 31) In a stunning showdown at the Cooper County Fair, a 12-year-old Steele boy was awarded the $1,000 prize in a carnival game after retired Circuit Court Judge Ruth Salzberg demonstrated that the game was rigged to deprive him of victory.

"It wasn't me who uncovered the deception, it was Wil," said Salzberg of the boy, Wilson Glenn David the Fifth. "He just needed a little help to make sure his claim was taken seriously."

As sheriff's deputies attempted to arrest fair owner F. James "Jimbo" Bates and an employee, Frances "Curly" Moffitt, an angry mob of fairgoers seized both men, first covering them in powdered sugar taken from the funnel cake vendor and then forcing them to act as targets in the water pistol "balloon bust" booth. Both men were sopping wet, sticky, and attracting flies when taken into custody after the arrival on scene of the sheriff's elite SWAT team, whose hostage negotiation specialist convinced the mob to let them go.

"Scoundrels! They deserve all that and more," said Diane Wallace, a Coop de Ville resident who was attending the fair with her children. "Imagine, trying to cheat people of what they won honestly."

The boy, who is homeschooled by his mother, said he had watched the game carefully since the fair opened Thursday but only realized Saturday night precisely how the carny was preventing people from earning the top prize, which is won by tossing three disks to completely cover a red spot.

"It was actually my friend Ann-Douglas who observed that the carny had a nylon thread tied between his ankle and the leg of the table where the spot is," said the boy, who is known as Wil. "When somebody had two good tosses, he'd give a sharp pull on the table leg just as the third disk was landing, to jostle everything around."

In a dramatic confrontation this reporter has never seen the likes of before, Salzberg, assisted by two sheriff's deputies, challenged the carny after Wil appeared to have won the game, demanding Moffitt step out from the booth. He complied after being ordered to do so by Dep. Liam Davidson, but had to remove his pants first. Davidson took the pants, and the fishing line attached to them, into police custody as evidence.

A similar dispute over the Cover the Spot game arose June 27, at the Livingston County Fair, when witnesses reported a Florida man had won the game only to be told by Moffitt seconds later that a small portion of the spot was still visible. Bates reportedly paid Hodson the $1,000 prize after one of Hodson's relatives produced a videotape showing a freeze-frame of the spot completely covered, followed by a sudden, minor shift a split second after the third disk had landed. Bates claimed at the time that he had fired the employee involved—Moffitt. Last night, Moffitt's employee nametag read "Carl" with the "u" from Curly apparently changed into an "a" and the "y" blacked out.

Bates and Moffitt were charged with multiple counts of larceny by deception and are being held without bail at the Cooper County Jail until their arraignment, scheduled for this morning.

"Mr. Bates has a record of leaving town when trouble arrives," Salzberg said, "so I asked my colleagues at the courthouse to make sure, this time, that the last we see of Mr. Bates isn't him waving good-bye to us from the caboose of his train."

Newspaper Carrier to Reporter: Tough Cookies

The phone rang all day at the Davids', and Wil had the supreme pleasure of answering it when the reporter from *The Caller* phoned, wanting an interview.

"How did *The Satellite Valley News* get this story before us?" he asked, clearly chuffed that he had been beaten on a big story on his own turf by a reporter from the next county.

"I called them," Wil admitted.

"Why did you do that?"

"I'll answer your questions as soon as your bosses reinstate home delivery to my town," Wil said, and hung up. That was fun, he thought.

The Associated Press also called. They had read Phoebe Flowers's story on the newswire. Wil answered all that reporter's questions except the one about what he planned to do with his thousand dollars.

"There's one other thing I'd like to mention. Our town is having a meeting tonight to talk about what we can do to get our local newspaper to keep delivering the paper here," Wil said.

"What do you mean?" the reporter asked.

"Our local paper announced last week that it isn't going to offer home delivery to our town anymore," Wil said. "Everybody here is really upset."

"Wow, did they give you a reason?"

"The circulation guy said we're too small for advertisers to care about reaching us."

"Harsh! I'll talk to my editor about it. Where's this meeting going to be?"

Wil gave her the details.

The whole family was going to the meeting, since Junior's update on the hairpin factory was the first item on the short, summertime agenda. Wil asked Sonny to save him a seat because he had a stop to make on his way there. Then he set out on his bike, which, thanks to Junior, looked as good as new.

He pedaled over to Madame Prévu's.

"I've been expecting you," she said from her perch in the porch swing, a green-eyed calico cat curled into her lap.

"I figured you might be," Wil said, smiling.

"Sit here," she said, patting the swing. "You have things on your mind."

Wil sat down and the cat jumped off, meowing.

"I just wanted to thank you and . . ." He knew he would have trouble getting the next thing out. He took a deep breath. "I wanted to apologize for not taking what you said very seriously at first."

"No apology is necessary, Wil of Steele. People routinely ignore my advice and, of course, they scoff at my practice.

You did neither. It just took a while for my guidance to get heard in your hardworking brain."

"I should've known better. For a long time, it was hard to get anybody in my house to listen to what I had to say."

"For instance?"

"Well, like, do you know the story about me not wanting to go to school?"

"I have heard that amusing tale, yes."

"But it wasn't funny to me. I mean, I really didn't belong there. The other kids made so much noise my head hurt. But nobody believed me. They just decided I was stubborn."

"This is the plight of being the youngest, I think," she said. "Have they grown out of it by now?"

"I think so." Wil nodded. "I never really did believe in wishes or luck till I met you. But I think the horseshoe really did help."

"Is that the only reason you came here? To apologize?"

"You already know it isn't, right?"

She smiled. "Yes."

"What I was wondering is, if you saw anything else about me—I mean, I'm about to do something that I think is the right thing but I'm a little nervous," he said.

"Ah."

"Do you already know what I'm planning?"

"Absolutely not, but I can see by the gravity of your demeanor that it involves personal sacrifice, no?"

Wil nodded. He couldn't look at her, but he could tell she was studying him.

"The vibrations in your aura tell me that what you are trying to do by making this sacrifice will succeed."

"They do?" Wil had not even known he had an aura.

"They do, but . . ." She held the swing steady so she could stand and Wil would not fall off.

"But?"

"But it never hurts to have luck." She reached above the door for the horseshoe. "Stand, please."

Wil got up and bent his head. Madame Prévu turned the horseshoe upside down over him. "Good luck, Wil of Steele. This time I am not completely certain you need it."

"Thanks, Madame P.," he said. "For a medium, I think you're extra-large."

She threw back her head and laughed. *"Merci beaucoup!"* she said when she recovered. "No one has ever considered me extra-large before."

"Got that from Sonny," he said, taking the porch steps in a single leap. Then he threw his leg across his bike and waved back at her before pedaling off into the slowly setting August sun.

Boys Plant Seed, Idea Takes Root

Wil had to wedge his bike between a lot of others at the rack outside Town Hall. The parking lot was full, too, in part because a long swath of it had been consumed by a huge satellite news van from KDKA-TV in Pittsburgh. He got a weird feeling in his stomach looking at it. Did I do that? Had the Associated Press reporter mentioned the Town Council meeting in her story about the Cover the Spot fraud? Could she have already written it and put it out on the wire? Or was it possible somebody in Pittsburgh read *The Satellite Valley News*?

Everyone was standing when he entered the room—reciting the Pledge of Allegiance. Wil hadn't been to any Town Council meetings before, but he was pretty sure they didn't normally attract this large a crowd. Every seat appeared to be taken. The pledge finished, people folded noisily into their chairs. He glimpsed Judge Salzberg and Ann-Douglas as they sat before he saw Sonny, down in front, waving to the spot he'd saved for Wil.

Wil had never loved his brother more than he did that day. Earlier, he had told Sonny what he planned to do at the meeting, and Sonny hadn't hesitated. "Count me in, Wil. I'll go through my sock drawer and see what I've got." A boy did not need to be the smartest kid in school if he had a heart the size of Sonny's. Wil was glad to have become friends with Madame Prévu, but he'd been lucky long before he met her.

"Are we giving something away and nobody told me?" said Mrs. Stinson, who, in her role as mayor, presided over the Town Council. Lots of people laughed. "I'm not sure how long our AC will hold out with this many people packed in here, so let's get right to business. First up is Junior David, who has an update on the hairpin factory."

Junior stood and walked to a podium centered in front of the dais. "Thank you, Margie. Last week I gave two people from the county Economic Development Council a tour of the factory. They were real impressed by how we've kept it up, and how well thought out it was, architecturally speaking, to begin with. They called it 'employee friendly.'"

"Except to the employees who were terminated," Señor Lopez Lopez said. He was a council member, too. "Which was all of them."

Junior nodded grimly. "Anyway, these folks see the possibility for light manufacturing, warehousing, maybe even telemarketing."

"Are those the people who call us while we're eating dinner?" asked Brad Norris, another council member.

"Or when you're in the shower, yes," Junior said.

"Oh, anything but that," Mr. Norris said.

"It's better than having your kids go hungry!" someone shouted from the audience.

Mayor Stinson rapped her gavel firmly once. "Let's hear Junior out, please."

"So here's the catch. They've got some prospective businesses looking to open in this area, but it won't be enough to provide them with a building and good workers. Most of these companies are now getting tax credits or financial incentives to locate somewhere. And these people from the Economic Development Council want to know how much towns that need businesses are willing to contribute. Some towns that own a building, like ours, are giving huge discounts on rent, or forgoing tax collection for a few years. If we want to be in the running, we've got to come up with something, too. These folks want some seed money up front to demonstrate our commitment."

Grumbling rippled through the audience like a wave. Mayor Stinson shook her head in disbelief. Señor Lopez said, "You informed them that it is not possible to get blood from the turnip?"

"I didn't put it that way, but, yeah, they know we have people out of work here so long that their unemployment's run out. But so do other towns. We can't decide we're not going to even try to raise some money just because it seems, well, cruel. I think we need to figure out what we can offer that will make us attractive."

"Junior's right," Mayor Stinson said. "We can grouse all we want about it but we need a business in that factory if our downtown is going to survive, and if our downtown dies, living here will be a lot less pleasant than it is now, agreed?"

"Let us challenge ourselves," Señor Lopez said. "Each of us must come up with an idea—something we could do without in the town budget so that money can be earmarked for this. Or some lagniappe that could be offered that would make us irresistible."

"What the heck's a lanyap?" Sonny whispered to Wil. "Is that like a lanyard?"

"I think it's like a tip," Wil whispered in return.

"A tip?" Sonny's face clouded. "You mean somebody might turn the hairpin factory into a restaurant?"

"Any member of the audience with an idea, we'd like to hear them, too," Mayor Stinson said.

Wil's palms were already sweating. He dried both hands on his shorts while he looked around the room to see if someone else was going to speak first. He swallowed to get his throat working before hesitantly standing.

"I'd like to say something, Mayor Stinson," he said, lifting his hand to catch her eye.

"Come to the microphone, Wil. You're up next anyway, but first—Jill Dixon from KDKA is here. This is your boy, Jill. Our local hero."

The TV reporter had been seated to the right of the audience. She stood now, as did her cameraman, who turned on a light so bright it made the people in the first two rows shield their eyes.

"For anybody who hasn't heard yet, Wil here, who you all know is also our new carrier, won himself a thousand dollars and got two crooks arrested at the fair last night."

The audience applauded warmly. Wil felt his face flush.

"Nice piece of detective work, Wil. If we had a police force, I'd put you in charge of the fraud unit." More laughs.

"Now, Wil's topic tonight is *The Caller.* I understand you got just about everybody's name on your petition."

"Actually, Mayor Stinson, before we finish with the hairpin factory, I'd like to say something about that," Wil said.

"We could use your fine brain on this problem, Wil. Go ahead."

"Sonny and I talked it over, and we'd both like to contribute to that seed money fund." He walked forward to the dais and handed Mayor Stinson a thick manila envelope. "That's one thousand four hundred and forty-six dollars."

"Oh, Wil," Mayor Stinson said. She paused, looking at her council for backup. "We can't take all your money."

"Just a thousand dollars of it is mine. The rest Sonny had in his sock drawer."

Sonny stood. "I got more stashed other places, Mayor Stinson. And that money came from all of you, anyway, fifty cents and a dollar at a time," he said, gesturing to his customers in the audience. "Wil told me his idea and right away I thought, 'I want to chip in for the seeds, too. I mean, after all, money doesn't grow on trees, but pears do.'"

There was a long silence while everyone in the council chambers tried to figure out what Sonny had said. After it went on too long, Mayor Stinson spoke up. "Well, I'm speechless."

"What fine young people," said Brad Norris, dabbing his eye with a tissue.

"Perhaps we should consider this a loan?" Señor Lopez proposed. "These boys have inspired me. I am on a fixed income, but I have bottomless faith in our town. I will match their contribution with the hope that someday I will be paid back. Perhaps it will be my heirs who collect, but I am willing."

"I don't have a thousand dollars, but I have a hundred," called Zachary Roberts, who had been fixing cars out of his garage since the hairpin factory closed. "Can anyone match that?"

"I certainly can," said Mayor Stinson.

"Me, too," said Brad Norris. That started an onslaught. The Bryants had fifty dollars to contribute, which the Bradys matched. Heather and Susan, who owned the beauty parlor, proposed a fund-raiser.

"We'll set aside a day and do your 'do for a donation," Heather said. Somebody produced a notepad, and a line formed to sign up. Mayor Stinson asked for a volunteer to keep a list of who was willing to pledge what, and several hands went up.

Wil tried to sneak away, but Jill Dixon from KDKA caught him. "Wow, I thought the story was the carnival game," she said, and began firing questions. Wil made Sonny come and stand beside him, and when he saw Ann-Douglas out of the corner of his eye, he waved her over, too, introducing her to the reporter.

"This is the person who really caught that carny cheating," he said. The reporter wanted details, and Wil happily stepped out of the spotlight. When she finished with Ann-Douglas, Wil approached. "Can I ask you one thing, Miss Dixon?"

"Of course."

"How did you find out about this meeting?"

"We got an e-mail." She flipped through the sheets of paper clamped to her clipboard. "Here it is. You can have it. I don't need it anymore. She sure was right!"

Wil took the printout.

To: 2newsdesk@KDKA-TV.com

From: FleursAbroad@sudamerinet.com

Subj: Not to be missed News Event of Great Interest and Importance

¿Do you want an exclusive news story that will rock the world of your viewers? A 12-year-old boy from Steele single-handedly uncovered a totally shady operation at the Cooper County Fair over the weekend. The cops put two felons in handcuffs, including the fair owner. ¿Don't believe me? Call my buddy Ruth Salzberg. She's a retired judge and she saw the whole thing. Her number's in the book.

You're not too late to get the scoop. The boy wonder himself, Wilson Glenn David the Fifth, will be at the Steele Town Council meeting at 7 p.m.

Tomorrow, I'm sending this message to the Post-Gazette, the Philadelphia Inquirer, and the New York Times, so get busy.

That Fleur, Wil thought. She could stir a hornet's nest from a continent away. He returned to his seat, as Mayor Stinson had finished appointing a "seed money" committee.

"Now, Wil," she said, just when he thought his fifteen minutes of fame had expired. "Let's talk about *The Caller.*"

He stood again.

"You have that petition with you?"

He pulled it from his back pocket.

"Frank Fernandez, is that you hiding in the back?"

Every head in the room turned to where Mayor Stinson was squinting. A man with a notebook was leaning against the wall, trying to make himself as small as possible.

"I'm only here to write about the Cover the Spot game," he said.

"Don't kill the messenger, folks, but that's Frank Fernandez from *The Caller,*" Mayor Stinson said. "C'mon up, Frank."

Frank looked like he'd rather impale himself on a sharp stick, but he did what he was told.

"Wil, give that petition to Frank," Mayor Stinson told him. "Now, Frank, we've always been very friendly people, haven't we?"

"Yes, Mayor Stinson," the reporter said. "Steele is the nicest town on my beat."

"Well, the party's over, Frank. You take this petition back to your bosses and tell them nobody from *The Caller* is welcome here unless they're going to bring us the paper, too. I can't keep you out—that's against the law—and you're free to quote whatever I say in a public meeting. But I, for one, am not taking calls from you or anybody else at the paper till they see fit to rescind this ridiculous decision." Her next remark was directed at the audience. "What say the rest of you?"

Judge Salzberg stood first. "I'll tell you what I say. We've taken some hard blows recently here in Steele."

"That's for sure!" someone shouted.

"But maybe this newspaper nonsense is the kick in the pants we needed. We ought to take more responsibility for what happens to us, and to our town. Maybe it's natural to avert our eyes because we're afraid. Afraid Steele is dying. But the truth is, nobody's gonna rescue this town except us."

"Hear, hear," someone said, and "She's right," someone else agreed.

"Sometimes the most powerful thing you can do is say 'No,'" Judge Salzberg continued. "'No, we're not going to let our town die.' And 'No, we're not going to sit on our hands when the newspaper consigns us to the dustbin.' When they let advertisers dictate who's entitled to information about what's going on in the world and in our own community, why, they're saying we count for nothing."

"They're wrong!" someone shouted.

Judge Salzberg made her way to the center aisle before she continued. "Take our paper away? Wil David said 'No,' and asked the rest of us to join the chorus. So, Mayor Stinson, what I have to say is this: Hip, hip, hooray for Wilson Glenn David the Fifth. Long live Wil of Steele!"

Wil had his head down, embarrassed, when Sonny and Trace put their hands under his armpits and lifted him onto their shoulders as everybody in the room—everybody in Steele, it seemed—rose to their feet and gave Wil a standing ovation.

Long-Held Goal Achieved!

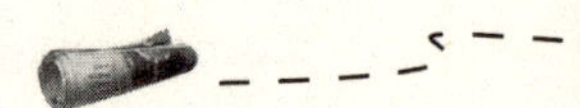

Wil sidearmed the paper with force so it skidded onto Mayor Stinson's porch just as she was opening her front door.

"Mornin', Wil!" she called.

He waved back before reaching for the next newspaper. The cooler morning air made his job easier. He was reminding himself to enjoy it, since Sonny had promised that the colder it got, the harder it was to get out of bed. Actually, what Sonny had said was, "You know what they say, Wil. It's always darkest right before the dawn of daylight saving time," but Wil knew what he meant. He wondered if there was any wider advantage to being fluent in Sonny-ese.

Oscar, the Suttles' dog, was waiting for him, as usual. Wil flung the paper deep into his yard, watching the dog go into his sprint before the paper had even landed. Then Wil quickly tossed a biscuit onto the sidewalk. He had figured out that Oscar wanted desperately to bring his owner the newspaper. By landing it on the porch, Wil was causing the little guy a great deal of frustration. The treat, which Oscar always went to retrieve after dropping the paper on the porch himself, was his tip for helping Wil ensure timely delivery of everybody's newspaper. Oscar never chased him anymore.

Today, however, Wil had extra reason to hustle. He had already overslept because he had stayed up late helping Magnolia with her new job. The hairpin factory had been bought, lock, stock, and metal fabricator, by a company that specialized in the sale of discount books—remainders, they were called. Somebody who worked for the company had seen a story about Wil which mentioned that the town's largest employer had shifted its manufacturing to Malaysia, putting people out of work and leaving the old factory empty. The book company had been looking for a distribution facility closer to the East Coast. The deal was sealed when they came to Steele for a tour and Junior introduced them to Magnolia, who impressed them with her encyclopedic knowledge of literature. She agreed to oversee the warehouse as long as she could also set up a small storefront within the factory for sales to the public. Magnolia couldn't bear to have all those books so close and not let her neighbors have a crack at them. She also knew that a good bookstore would draw people to Steele, so she negotiated a sublease for Junior, who converted the former employee cafeteria, a space that opened onto a leafy patio facing the town green, into a restaurant serving the warehouse's employees and the public. Junior's on Mane, he had named it.

"Won't people worry that there might be hair in the soup if you call it that?" Sonny worried.

"Rabbit soup?" Junior asked. "I'm not planning on serving that ever."

The Davids had never worked harder, or been busier. But their new jobs involved things they loved—food and books and keeping their hometown alive.

Wil flung a paper at Ann-Douglas's door. The Harvest Dance was only a week away, and Ann-Douglas was over at his house every afternoon trying to teach him to waltz.

"They're not going to play this kind of music, Ann-Douglas," he insisted.

"It never hurts to be ready, Wil," she said. "At some point in your life, a waltz will come in handy." He had decided not to fight her and, so far, had stepped on, but not broken, her toes many, many times. Not on purpose, of course, although it could be construed as a measure of revenge.

The Caller, naturally, had changed its mind about the route through Steele. They might have reversed course even before a feature story on Wil ran in *People* magazine. The tone of the story suggested *The Caller* was run by unfeeling clods. Right after the article appeared, Double-G finally responded to Wil's original e-mail, saying that, during the hectic period following the sale of *The Caller* to News, Inc., he had misinterpreted a directive from the new management team. Yeah, right, Wil thought. But he let it go.

After getting that e-mail, Wil's first act had not been to rush right home and break the good news to his family and his customers. Instead he had recalculated how long it would take him to save enough money for a laptop. But he needn't have. The first paycheck Magnolia got, she and Wil drove to one of those big-box stores in Pittsburgh and bought Wil the laptop he wanted. He got it the very same week he started school in Coop de Ville. With Magnolia and Junior both out of the house during the day, they mildly wondered whether Wil would consider going to school instead of staying home by himself.

"Okay," Wil answered.

"Okay?" Magnolia and Junior exclaimed in unison.

"Okay. I'll try it," he said, not being able to suppress a smile when he saw the shocked looks on his parents' faces.

Now, after school, and waltzing, Wil was working on his first big computer project—creating a Web site for the town of Steele. The typewriter Fleur had sent him from South America had not yet even been taken out of the box, because everybody in Steele was keen to get the Web site up and running. Mayor Stinson wanted space to regularly update residents on municipal news. Judge Salzberg asked for space to blog about big issues, like social justice, participatory democracy, and the proper proportion of beans to beef in a pot of chili. Señor Lopez Lopez was only too happy to contribute a riddle of the day, and Wil even had a foreign correspondent who was thrilled almost beyond words to finally have a reliable forum for her opinions. The only snag was that Fleur was currently living at the top of a tree, to protest deforestation of the Brazilian jungle. Sometimes it took a while to get e-mails from her.

Ann-Douglas contributed photos. Wil planned to include a link to the day's specials at Junior's on Mane, and Magnolia provided reading recommendations—a way of advertising her new bookstore, which she named Remainders of the Day, even though her sons thought that an odd choice. "Literate people will understand," she insisted. All of the site's elements were coming together in clean, but snazzy, fashion, thanks to Trace, who had put down his pencil to learn Web design. That was the future, after all.

But that morning Wil wasn't thinking about the digital horizon. Or about how it was possible that, even after changing *The Caller*'s mind once, it was still likely he could be, if not the last newspaper boy in America, then the very last one in Steele. He brought his laptop to the library now so he could spend all the time he wanted online, reading news, playing awesome games, chatting with the physicists.

No, he was thinking about the school bus, and how it would arrive at Town Hall to pick up everybody going to the middle or high school, and how Mrs. Goggins, the driver, really didn't care that you slept in because you were up late teaching yourself how to write html code. The bus left the town green at six-forty-five whether you were on it or not.

So, as the last paper flew out of his hands and onto Señor Lopez's balcony, Wil did not coast. He pumped his legs and flew.

"He's here!" said Sonny, who was waiting for him on the back porch. "I think you did it!"

Wil smiled as he wheeled his bike into the garage. Wow! He hadn't been thinking of his time at all.

"Impossible," Junior said, stepping out the back door with a stopwatch in his hands.

"What's it say?" Sonny asked.

Junior turned the watch to show him the readout: thirty-five minutes and fifty-one seconds.

"Congratulations, Wil," Junior said, a huge grin spreading across his face. "You just beat my record."

Notes on

The Beginning of the Paper Clip

and

The End of the Newspaper Boy

(and Girl)

In a time of mind-boggling technological advancement (you might be reading this on your iPhone) it's hard to imagine that a little more than a hundred years ago the humble paper clip was considered revolutionary.

Indeed, many people sought to claim credit for inventing it. To write this novel I did some research into the paper clip's somewhat murky origins, but the history presented in Wil David's report is a mix of fact and fiction. The real story behind this ubiquitous invention is not as tidy.

In actual history, the earliest version of a paper clip was called a "ticket fastener," patented in 1867 by Samuel B. Fay. Fay meant for his device to be used to attach price tickets to clothing but mentioned in his patent application that it could also be used to hold papers together. The first patent for a product specifically called a paper clip was granted to a Pennsylvanian, Matthew Schooley, in 1898. However, Schooley's paperwork mentions other clips of slightly different design that were already on the market, so it's hard to dub him Father of the Paper Clip. At approximately the same historical moment Schooley was twisting wire, Cornelius Brosnan of Massachusetts was unveiling a slightly different design. He called his the Konaclip. And then there's the inventor that my fictional character, Wil David, mentions in his report on the history of Steele: William Middleton of Connecticut, a real person who designed a clip and a wire-forming machine that could mass-produce it. An office products company, Cushman and Denison, purchased Middleton's patent and trademarked the name GEM for its clip, although by 1907 there was also a British firm, Gem Manufacturing Ltd., exporting clips to the United States that had the same oval-within-an-oval design.

Now: Forget all that if you live in Norway, where people will assure you that hometown hero Johan Vaaler is the true inventor of the paper clip. In 1899, Vaaler received a patent for several possible paper clip shapes, including one similar to the Gem. Norwegian pride in Vaaler's invention led them to adopt the paper clip as a symbol of nationalism during World War II. To protest the Nazi occupation of their country, Norwegians affixed paper clips to their coats as a form of protest. Today there is a 23-foot tall statue of a paper clip in Oslo which pays homage to Vaaler.

Of course, the clip "invented" in my novel by Wil's great-grandfather, like Wil himself, springs in part from this research but mostly from my imagination. To learn more about the real stories behind many simple products we take for granted in our lives, I recommend reading *The Evolution of Useful Things*, by Henry Petroski.

By the way, Mr. Petroski was also a paperboy! He delivered *The Long Island Press* in Queens, New York during the 1950s. (Walt Disney was a paperboy, too—in Kansas City, Missouri. He reportedly hated getting up early in the cold to do his route.) Unlike paper clips, however, paperboys and girls may be losing their usefulness in today's world. Like Mr. Petroski, I also delivered *The Long Island Press*, until the paper shut its afternoon edition in the early 1970s. The trend away from offering afternoon and evening editions of many papers limited the number of delivery routes available to kids. Moreover, flinging papers from a bike in the early morning darkness is an activity that raises safety concerns with people like, say, your parents.

But the biggest reason for the demise of the "youth carrier," which is the term the industry uses, has to do with a fundamental shift in the way papers are distributed. Once upon a time, it was common to see big trucks with the name of the local newspaper painted on each side. These were the trucks, like Manny's in my novel, that brought the papers to the carriers. For the past two decades, newspapers have moved away from owning a fleet of trucks to operating a big distribution center where carriers come to pick up the papers they need for their route. This kind of system pretty much requires the carrier have an automobile rather than a bike. Since 1994, when larger newspapers started moving toward the distribution center model, the percentage of carriers who are adults has grown from 42.5 percent to 81.3 percent (in 2006) of the carrier workforce. (The 18.7 percent who are youth carriers are primarily employed by smaller newspapers.) Bigger routes, completed by adults in station wagons or minivans, have become the norm.

That doesn't mean you shouldn't treat yourself at least once to the thrill of tossing a newspaper from a moving bike and landing it smack on the doorstep. Try it with the newspaper your family gets—quick!—while they are still delivering one to your neighborhood.

ACKNOWLEDGMENTS *The author thanks the Davidson In-house Focus Group for their bottomless enthusiasm about Wil's story, which manifested itself in much patient listening, solid suggestions, and selfless offers to appear in the movie version.*

Deep gratitude is also extended to Annabelle Hoffman and Amelia Lawrence for reading the story in manuscript and giving me their thoughtful critiques, and to Ann-Douglas Vaughn for letting me borrow her name. The real Ann-Douglas is also a blond photographer, but she is not the least bit pesky.

The story benefited tremendously from the feedback of Mrs. Marjorie Stinson's fifth grade class ('08) at St. Andrew's Episcopal School in Newport News, Virginia. If I have left out anyone's name, let me know. I will get you in the next book.